Shep in the Victorio War

by Don DeNevi

TEXAS REVIEW PRESS
HUNTSVILLE, TEXAS

FIRST EDITION

Requests for permission to acknowledge material from this work should be sent to:

Permissions
Texas Review Press
English Department
Sam Houston State University
Huntsville, TX 77341-2146

author photo: by Scott Jenstad at the Huntington Library, San Marino, California
cover design: Kim Davis

Library of Congress Cataloging-in-Publication Data

Names: DeNevi, Don, 1937- author.
Title: Shep in the Victorio War / by Don DeNevi.
Description: First edition. | Huntsville, Texas : Texas Review Press, 2018. |
    Summary: "During the summer of 1880, amid the searing heat of the
    Chihuahuan Desert of West Texas and northern Mexico, Chief Victorio led
    his band of Mescalero and Warm Springs Apaches in a last, desperate exodus
    from a disease-ridden, barren reservation. Raiding cattle and horses to
    survive, Victorio and his people eluded pursuers on both sides of the Rio
    Grande, as the US Army, the Texas Rangers, and the Mexican territorial
    militia combined forces to ferret out and eliminate the fugitive Apaches.
    Into the midst of the authentic historical backdrop of what became known
    as the Victorio War, author Don DeNevi places Shep, a black German
    Shepherd rescued and loved by Joseph Andrews and William Wiswall, two
    adventurers from the Colorado mining country. Shep forms an inexplicable
    bond with the Apache chief that leads Wiswall and Andrews into an
    unexpected and uncomfortable role. The imagined events of Shep in the
    Victorio War follow immediately upon those portrayed in DeNevi's earlier
    novel, Faithful Shep: The Story of a Hero Dog and the Nine Texas Rangers
    Who Saved Him"-- Provided by publisher.
Identifiers: LCCN 2017059918 (print) | LCCN 2018004516 (ebook) | ISBN
    9781680031607 (ebook) | ISBN 9781680031591 | ISBN 9781680031591¬(pbk.)
Subjects: LCSH: Victorio, Apache Chief, -1880--Fiction. | Mescalero
    Indians--Fiction. | Warm Spring Apache Indians--Fiction. | Apache
    Indians--Wars--Fiction. | Dogs--Fiction. | Human-animal
    relationships--Fiction. | United States--Territorial expansion--Fiction. |
    Frontier and pioneer life--Texas, West--Fiction. | Chihuahuan
    Desert--Fiction. | Texas, West--Fiction. | Mexico, North--Fiction. |
    LCGFT: Historical fiction.
Classification: LCC PS3604.E536 (ebook) | LCC PS3604.E536 Sh 2018 (print) |
    DDC 813/.6--dc23
LC record available at https://lccn.loc.gov/2017059918

A dedication

Lest they be lost among the proliferating western writers of our time, this quiet remembrance acknowledges two of our nation's most revered storytellers of the American West:

Pearl Zane Grey (1872–1939),

for *Betty Zane* (1903),

Riders of the Purple Sage (1912),

The Vanishing American (1925),

and so many other romances;

And . . .

Stewart Edward White (1873–1946)

for *The Long Rifle* (1932),

Ranchero (1933), and

Folded Hills (1934).

For those of us who yearn for exemplars, there are no finer.

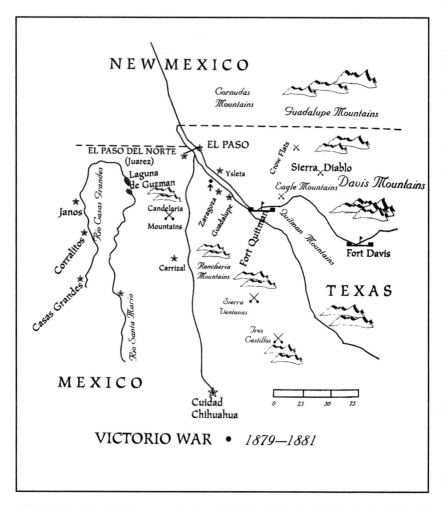

NEW MEXICO

Cornudas Mountains

Guadalupe Mountains

EL PASO DEL NORTE
(Juarez)

EL PASO

Crow Flats ×

Ysleta

Sierra Diablo

Laguna de Guzman

Eagle Mountains *Davis Mountains*

Janos

Rio Casas Grandes

Candelaria

Mountains

Zaragoza

Guadalupe

Quitman Mountains

Fort Quitman

Fort Davis

Corralitos

Carrizal

Rancheria Mountains

Casas Grandes

Rio Santa Maria

Sierra Ventanas

TEXAS

Tres Castillos ×

MEXICO

Cuidad
Chihuahua

0   25   50   75

VICTORIO WAR • *1879–1881*

Map courtesy Jerry D. Thompson, originally published in Into the Far Wild Country: True Tales of
the Old Southwest *(by G. W. Baylor, ed. Jerry D. Thompson; Texas Western Press, 1996).*

Shep in the Victorio War

Chapter 1

"**H**ell's bells! Why do I have to be the one to tell him?" William Wiswall said. "This wasn't my idea alone, you know!"

"Well, I just thought . . . with your gifts of expression . . ." Joseph Andrews said. He wouldn't meet Wiswall's eyes.

They sat on a low adobe wall fronting the dusty road in front of the headquarters of Company A, Frontier Battalion, Texas Rangers. A scraggly, yet determined mulberry tree shaded them from the July sun. They watched an ox wain trundle slowly past on the road. Driven by a Mexican who trudged along beside his phlegmatic beast of burden, the wain was stacked to the top of the sideboards with mesquite wood cut into uniform two-foot lengths, likely harvested from the thickets lining the drainage of the Rio Grande, farther to the southeast. The driver held a switch in his hand, and now and again he flicked it against the flank of the brown-speckled steer. As far as Wiswall could tell, the driver's lackadaisical urging made no alteration in the speed of either man or beast. The woodcutter was probably on his way to the market square in El Paso to sell the mesquite for a few cents per rick. The ox trod so slowly that the solid oak disks of the wheels barely raised any dust in the hot, still air.

"I guess this means you're still convinced in your own mind about south California."

Andrews nodded. "I believe I am, yes."

"Well, I guess it isn't going to get any easier. But all the same . . ."

"He has been more than generous, there's no question," Andrews said. "They took us in like long-lost family. They have included us as full members of their company. Telling the lieutenant we plan to leave will not be pleasant."

"I sure appreciate all you're doing to make this less difficult," Wiswall said, giving his partner a sour look. "This is all your fault, anyway, Shep," he said, gently nudging with the toe of his boot the black shepherd dog that lay at his feet, panting in the heat. "If you hadn't jumped out of the wagon when we tried to leave the first time . . ."

Andrews smiled at the memory. "Hopped out and ran back up the hill toward Ysleta, and stopped to look back at us as if to say, 'What in tarnation is wrong with you fellows, anyway?' Nothing for us to do but turn around and follow him back here."

"Damned dog made up our minds for us," Wiswall said. "So what do you think, Shep? Should we chuck it all in and go to south California? What do you say, old boy?"

"Just stands to reason," Andrews said. "Once the railroads join up, lots of people are going to come west. They say the climate is perfect out there; they say you can damn near stick a dry twig in the ground and it'll grow. Why not get out there and stake a claim before the whole place gets priced out of our reach?"

"Your logic is as sound as ever," Wiswall said. "We've been all over this, three ways from Sunday. I couldn't agree more. It certainly seems a more likely prospect than buying burros in Texas and taking them back to the mines in Colorado."

"That venture never did really pay out, did it?" Andrews said. "But we sure learned plenty."

"And gained the friendship of some of the finest men in the world," Wiswall said.

Andrews nodded, thoughtfully toeing the dust in the shade of the mulberry.

"All right." Wiswall sighed, stood up from the wall, and straightened his hat on his head. He looked back toward the Ranger station at the broad front porch spanning the front of Lieutenant George Wythe Baylor's house, which doubled as company headquarters. Inside that house, the previous January, they had sat at the dining room table and eaten a delightful meal prepared by Mrs. Baylor, even as her husband had tried in vain to dissuade them from trying to return to their Colorado home by a route that eventually resulted in the theft of their horses by Chief Victorio's marauding Apaches. Later, standing in the large front parlor of that same house, Wiswall and Andrews had watched in amazement as the men of Company A volunteered to ride east, into the desert, and rescue a cold and hungry Shep from the abandoned stagecoach station, surrounded by hostile Apaches, where Andrews and Wiswall had been forced to leave him. In that same parlor, the two of them had subsequently accepted the role of honorary Texas Ranger offered to them by Lieutenant Baylor, when they—at Shep's prompting—had opted to stay in Ysleta rather than return to Ouray County, Colorado, and their jobs as mining engineers.

Now Wiswall was going to walk in there and tell Lieutenant Baylor that, all things considered, he and Andrews were going to take their leave and follow the siren call of south California riches.

"Want me to come with you?" Andrews said.

"No, that's all right. You and Shep stay here; I'll let you know how it goes."

Wiswall took a deep breath, straightened his shoulders, and started walking toward the house. He heard the sound of running feet, approaching from across the dusty yard that separated the main house from the barracks. He turned just in time to see Sergeant James Gillett, Baylor's second-in-command, vaulting up the steps and onto the broad porch.

"Excuse me, William," the sergeant said, out of breath. "But I've got an important dispatch for the lieutenant." He quickly knocked on the front door.

Lieutenant Baylor's tall, solid frame filled the doorway. "Sergeant?"

"Sir, this dispatch just arrived by courier from Colonel Grierson, with the Tenth Cavalry. I've ridden from Fort Bliss to bring it to you."

Baylor tore open the envelope and unfolded the letter. Wiswall watched as he scanned the text. He gave Sergeant Gillett a thoughtful look, then re-read the dispatch.

"Assemble the men," he said when he finished reading. "Tell them to prepare for a two-week patrol. Gather up here in about a half-hour, and I'll present the situation to them."

"Yes, sir," Gillett said. He wheeled around and nearly collided with Wiswall. "Pardon me again, William." He ducked past the stocky Wiswall, clattered down the steps, and strode quickly across the yard toward the barracks.

"Forgive me, Lieutenant, but what was that all about?" Wiswall said.

Baylor was staring down at the letter again. He looked up at Wiswall. "It's Victorio, William. Colonel Grierson has received intelligence on his movements from Colonel Terrazas, over in Chihuahua. They believe he's headed for Eagle Spring, to the east of Fort Quitman. We're going to help the army and the Mexican militia track him down—for the last time, I hope."

"I see."

"Was there something you needed William?"

Wiswall, lost in thought, realized that Baylor had asked him a question. "Oh, no, not at all, Lieutenant. I'll just go tell Andrews that we need to get ready to ride."

"William, you and Joseph are here of your own free will, as honorary members of this company, only. You are not obliged to go with us on this patrol."

Wiswall stared evenly at the lieutenant. "You weren't obliged to ride into certain danger to save our dog."

Baylor looked away. "That was different. The men and I went willingly."

"And that is how Andrews and I will go on this patrol—along with Shep. We mean to see it through." He stared away, toward the east. "There are things about Victorio and his people that I would still like to understand. And it sounds like time is running out."

Baylor nodded. "That is possible, William."

Wiswall turned away. "That's what I figure, Lieutenant. And I imagine that Andrews and Shep will view it in the same light. We'll see you back here in thirty minutes or so."

Chapter 2

"Lieutenant Flipper and his patrol discovered Victorio's advance guard, not long after they crossed the Rio Grande, southwest of Van Horn's Wells," Baylor said. "Flipper and his three troopers rode nearly a hundred miles in less than a day to bring this intelligence to their commander, Captain Gilmore, who forwarded the information to Colonel Grierson.

"From the position and direction of the Apaches, Colonel Grierson has made the logical assumption that they were making for Eagle Spring, and that Victorio's main band will soon follow. Units of the Tenth Cavalry are being mobilized from Fort Davis in order to intercept Victorio. We are requested to rendezvous with the Tenth and assist in any engagements with Victorio that might occur."

Andrews watched as Shep circulated among the men gathered to listen to the briefing. The black dog paused long enough by each man to have his head scratched and his withers patted, before moving on to the next. Andrews shook his head and smiled. In the six months they had been here, Shep had become nearly the most famous member of the Ranger troop—as well known here and in El Paso as any of the men, including their commander and Sergeant Gillett.

Andrews would never forget watching the dog as he and Wiswall went out to speak to Victorio, standing on the bleak plain surrounding the Crow Spring station. The chief and his men had the Ranger patrol completely surrounded, yet, when Wiswall told him that they had come to Crow Spring for no purpose other than to rescue Shep, Victorio had allowed them to return unmolested to Ysleta. It was the most uncanny moment Andrews had ever experienced, and he did not expect to ever live through another like it.

Back in January, when they had left Ysleta, intending to return to Ouray County, one of Victorio's braves had met them by the roadside. Ignoring the certainty of imprisonment and the likelihood of death had he been apprehended, he had traveled all the way from Victorio to bring a final—what? Greeting? Blessing?—to Shep. By the time Shep bolted from the wagon, and he and Wiswall had turned around to go back to Ysleta, the Apache warrior-messenger was gone—as if he had never been there. *Strange experiences seem to multiply where you're concerned, old Shep*, Andrews thought.

Simon Olguin had been there, too, Andrews recalled, standing with the Apache whom he would have fought to the death, had they met in other circumstances. The Tigua Indian scout was one of the few other people who seemed to share the sort of mystical bond with Shep that he and Wiswall had, since they had rescued the dog from death in a lion baiting pit at Fort Sill.

It had been about three months since Olguin's death in an Apache ambush at Vieja Pass, down in Presidio County. Simon had tried in vain to warn the commander of the army detachment he was with, but the inexperienced lieutenant had insisted on bivouacking in the canyon near a spring. As Olguin had foreseen, Apaches had infiltrated the heights above the canyon floor. Only one enlisted man escaped to bring back the report. Shep had refused food and water for three days. None of them understood why until the news reached Ysleta from Fort Bliss, but Shep already knew.

Simon, I dearly wish you were with us on this patrol, Andrews thought. Aniceto, Simon's nephew, had more or less assumed his uncle's place as scout for the Ranger battalion. He was young, but very steady.

Baylor finished his briefing and the men dispersed to ready their kits for the ride. They were leaving before dark, Baylor had said.

As Andrews headed for the barracks, a movement caught his peripheral vision. Sergeant Gillett and Helen, the older of Lieutenant Baylor's two daughters, stood just around the corner of the house and were apparently engaged in a very deep conversation. When Helen turned her face toward him, Andrews quickly looked away. Gillett's interest in Helen Baylor was hard to miss; it had been increasing since the time the sergeant had originally accompanied the Baylor family on their long trek to Ysleta from San Antonio a year before. From what Andrews could tell, Miss Helen did not at all mind Gillett's attentions. *Parting is such sweet sorrow*, he thought. *As long as it is followed by a reunion, of course.* Continuing toward the barracks, Andrews renewed his promise to himself to avoid romantic entanglements until such time as his life was more predictable. *Or at least until I get back from this little ride with my scalp still anchored to my skull.*

Wiswall met him outside the barracks, leading a buckskin gelding and a blue roan mare. "I figured you'd want Pancho to start out on," he said, handing Andrews the buckskin's lead. "And I was able to talk Lloyd out of Mousey, for once."

"Thanks for saddling them. Is the rest of the gear still under the bunks?"

Wiswall nodded. "Except for the cartridges we bought yesterday for the Sharps and the Winchester. Those are still where we left them, in the tack room."

"All right. I'll swing by there and pick them up. Don't want to run out of bullets."

"I'm just going to drop this letter off, over at the stagecoach station; I'll be back here within the hour."

"Saying your last goodbyes to Annie?" Andrews said.

Wiswall wouldn't look at him. "Your humor is, as usual, sorely lacking."

Andrews gave a low chuckle. "You reckon this letter will be the one she answers? I hope you gave her my best."

"I tried my damnedest to avoid mentioning you at all."

Andrews laughed. "Go on with you, then. I'll put together as much of your kit as I can and make sure Mousey gets a good drink."

Victorio stood on the rocky bluff as the east began to gray toward dawn. Behind him, he could hear the sounds of his braves gathering up their weapons and catching the ponies they would ride today. In the ravine, shielded by scrub oak and ocotillo, a couple of the horses nickered low.

He was worried about his band. It was still a long way to the water they aimed for, at the place the whites called Rattlesnake Spring. It would have been much better to stop at Eagle Spring, close to the place they crossed the river from Mexico. But Victorio knew with a certainty he could not explain that if they went to the closer water, the bluecoats would be there waiting.

Instead, he had taken his people north, along the baking western slopes of the Sierra Diablo. It was hot and dry, and the water at Rattlesnake Spring was still a difficult half-day's ride away. But it was better to drink tired and thirsty than to die trying to reach the closer water. If they traveled quickly, they could drink and water their animals, then move on into the concealment of the Guadalupe Mountains, where the bluecoats would be hard-pressed to follow.

Hearing the sound of a moccasin against stone, he turned to see Kaytennae climbing toward him from the ravine where they had camped.

"Bidu-ya, the people are ready to travel," the brave said. "Bodaway has readied your pony, also."

"Give my son my thanks," Victorio said. "I am glad that the son of Holds His Horse is holding his horse."

Kaytennae gave a slow smile.

"How long do you think the Chihenne can live like this, Kaytennae?" Victorio said, looking away across the arid crags, brightening with the rising light. "How long can we take horses and cattle from the ranchos of the whites? How many times can we cross the river into Mexico to find rest from the pursuit of the bluecoats?"

"The Chihenne were starving and sick on the reservation at San Carlos, Bidu-ya," Kaytennae said. "It is better to live on the backs of our ponies, taking what we need, than to keep listening to the lies of the people who made us leave the place of our ancestors."

"For the warriors this is true, Kaytennae. But what about our women? What about our little ones? What about my granddaughter, Liluye, and the others?"

Kaytennae was silent for a while. "It is hard for

them, yes." He looked up at Victorio. "But even if life is short and hard, is it not better to be free? And the Chiricahua and Mescalero who ride with us—do they not say the same?"

"We are running out of room, Kaytennae," Victorio said, still peering across the desolate landscape. "The whites keep coming. We raid their stagecoaches, kill their people, and take their horses, and still they send more stagecoaches, more people, more horses, more guns. They build ranchos and towns and think that the land belongs to them. They do not think there is any place for the Chihenne, the Chiricahua, the Mescalero, or the Jicarilla, for any of the *nideh*—the people.

"And on the reservation, I heard them talk about their iron road. They build trails for their steam trains, so that they can bring even more people to this land, so that they can build more ranchos, more towns."

Victorio, whose name in his own tongue was Biduya—"Holds His Horse"—looked at his second-in-command. "There are too many of them, Kaytennae. They are too hungry. They will not stop until they have eaten everything. They will leave nothing behind for us."

After a long time, Kaytennae said, "What is to be done, then?"

Victorio gave the brave a sad smile. "Ride north. Drink. And then go into the mountains. Today, Kaytennae, that is what is to be done." He turned away from the edge of the bluff and followed Kaytennae back toward the camp, where his people waited. "Tell Liluye to come to me, Kaytennae. I want her to ride with me today. I want to tell her a story."

"Which one?"

Victorio smiled. "I think I will tell her about White-Painted Woman, when Child of the Water was born."

Chapter 3

Shep trotted along, tongue hanging out, about twenty feet in front of Aniceto Olguin. Wiswall tilted his hat brim down against the sun as he peered at the dog. "Well, he hasn't relinquished his customary spot in the lead since we left Ysleta last night," he said.

Ranger George Lloyd, trotting along beside Wiswall, chuckled. "I don't reckon Aniceto minds having him out there. Between that Tigua's eyes and Shep's ears and nose, I allow it ought to be hard for even old Vic to surprise us."

They were approaching the dilapidated remains of Fort Quitman, expecting to meet there with elements of Colonel Grierson's Tenth Cavalry. "I hear tell the army's talking about re-garrisoning Quitman," Lloyd said, studying the small scattering of adobe buildings as the Ranger column drew near. "Have to say, I'd hate to be one of the poor cusses that has to stay here. No worse situation in the country than Quitman, from what I've heard."

"Didn't it get burned back in '77?" Wiswall said.

"Yep. Bunch of angry Mexicans from San Elizario, mad about the Salt War. Most of them vamoosed across the Rio Grande when they heard the Ninth Cavalry was on the way, but they torched Quitman on their way out."

"What's going on there?" Wiswall said, pointing. A figure was running toward Aniceto on foot, waving his arms and shouting. The runner paused when he saw Shep, but he was still attempting to convey some message to the Tigua scout.

Up ahead, Lieutenant Baylor spurred his mount quickly forward, closely followed by Sergeant Gillett. The two cantered to Aniceto and conferred for a moment. Baylor shouted something, and Shep trotted back to stand beside Baylor's horse. Dismounting, Baylor strode forward to talk with the runner from Fort Quitman.

The rest of the Rangers gathered up in a loose group around Gillett, Aniceto, and Shep.

"What do you reckon, Sergeant?" one of the men said.

"That soldier came from the fort," Aniceto said. "I think he has news about Victorio."

A moment later, they saw Baylor turn and begin striding quickly back toward the column. "Boys," he said when he got close enough, "Colonel Grierson has gone ahead of us. We've been directed to continue scouting toward Eagle Spring until we meet up with him. So, let's water the horses and refill our canteens and then ride east with all dispatch."

The Rangers went to the water troughs at the ramshackle fort and their mounts quickly submerged their muzzles, slurping loudly. The men refilled their canteens and water skins from the nearby hand pump, and a few of them pulled dried beef from their saddlebags as they waited for the call to remount and ride out.

Within twenty minutes, they were jogging east along the San Antonio–El Paso Mail Coach trail. Heat wrinkled the air above the arid terrain, its dreary expanse relieved only by outcroppings of ocotillo, creosote, and broomstick-straight stalks of lechuguilla sprouting from their bases of spiny leaves.

"If memory serves," Andrews said, now riding beside Wiswall, "we're bearing more or less along the path that brought us here to begin with."

"I seem to recall a rather thrilling interlude involving a camel and a couple of spooked horses that we enjoyed somewhere hereabout," Wiswall said.

"You might have enjoyed it," Andrews said. "But you weren't the one who ended up sitting in the dirt with a banged-up shoulder."

"Happier times, partner. Happier times."

About an hour later they reached Eagle Spring, situated in a canyon pass through the Eagle Mountains. "This place has been ruined by Indians more times than I can remember," Gillett said to Andrews and Wiswall as they neared the broken-down adobe hut, squatting beside a snaggle-toothed stone corral. "They've been coming here for the water since time immemorial, and when the Jackass Mail put a station here, it didn't slow them down one bit." He gestured to the surrounding terrain. "Just look at all these gullies and canyons, around here. There's no way on God's green earth to adequately guard them all. No wonder the Apaches can sneak in here, any time they want."

"Well, they don't appear to be here now," Andrews said. "Apparently Colonel Grierson's intelligence was wrong."

"More likely, Victorio smelled a rat," one of the men said, pulling up beside the sergeant and the partners. "Aniceto is casting about for sign, and I'll wager you a plug of good tobacco he don't see nothing."

A few minutes later Baylor called them all together. "Doesn't look like either the cavalry or the Apaches have been here," he said. "As far as I understand Colonel Grierson's orders, we're to continue scouting east until we make contact with either the Indians or the army. Let's hope it's the latter. Water your mounts and yourselves, and let's press on—and keep your carbines close to hand."

"I don't much care for our orders," one of the men said in a low voice, standing beside his horse as it drank from the spring-fed cistern beside the corral. "We're getting awful far out into the countryside, with just the handful of us and no idea where Victorio is keeping hisself."

"Well, all things being equal," Wiswall said, filling his canteen, "I'd rather be riding with twelve other well-armed Rangers than headed back to Fort Quitman alone."

"That's so," the Ranger agreed, grudgingly.

They rode on, as the sun began casting long shadows along the canyon floors. As they were drawing near a place called Eighteen Mile Water Hole, Aniceto suddenly held up an arm. Baylor halted the column. The men nervously eyed the surrounding bluffs and fingered the triggers of their weapons as the Tigua guide dismounted and began peering closely at the ground, circling slowly.

"Shod horses here, maybe two days ago," he said, finally.

"Cavalry, then," Baylor said.

"Apache ponies, too, about the same time."

"Did they fight?" Gillett asked.

"Can't tell," Aniceto said. "No casings, no spent arrows. Maybe Victorio passed unseen."

"Which way did the Apaches go?" Baylor said.

Aniceto studied the ground some more. He pointed south. "There. Army, too."

Baylor and Gillett looked at each other. "If they went back into Mexico, we've come on a wild goose chase," Gillett said.

"Aniceto says the cavalry followed them, so we should, too, I suspect. Maybe this is where Flipper and his patrol picked up their trail. Maybe we ought to push along as fast as we can, in case there's a battle shaping up."

Gillett shrugged. "Likely worth a try, Lieutenant. That's as good as any idea I've got, for certain."

Baylor nodded. "Aniceto, lead on. Let's stick with the sign and see where it takes us."

The Rangers rode slowly along the road for several miles until they came to Bass Canyon, where Baylor called another halt.

"Don't need to be a Tigua to see what happened here," Andrews said. Wiswall gave a low whistle.

The telegraph line that ran along the mail road had been cut, and several poles had been pulled from the ground and dragged for several yards. The glass insulators were smashed.

"Apaches cross here," Aniceto said, peering at the ground. "Many."

Baylor had the Rangers dismount; he and Gillett conferred for a long time with the scout. After a few minutes, he called the men together.

"Aniceto says a large band—maybe two hundred horses—came up from the south and crossed here. They tore down the telegraph line and kept going north, toward the Carrizos. He says their sign is more recent than what we were following from Eighteen Mile Water Hole."

"Lieutenant, do you suppose that first bunch was the outriders that Lieutenant Flipper first reported, and this here is the main band?" Gillett said.

"It seems likely," Baylor said.

"What about heading on in to Van Horn's Wells?" George Lloyd said. "Do you reckon we could pick up any word about Grierson's movements there?"

Baylor thought for a moment. "Possibly. But I believe we ought to follow this trail north. It seems pretty clear that this is Victorio's main force. If Grierson comes upon them, or they come upon Grierson, there's going to be a fight—maybe the decisive fight. And we need to be on hand to do our part."

The lieutenant looked around at the men, giving them a chance to speak. After a few seconds of silence, he said, "All right, then. Let's mount up."

They struck north, across the plains fronting the eastern flanks of the Sierra Diablo range. Night fell, and stars speckled the sky.

"Not much moon tonight, boys. Let's not push the horses too hard," Gillett called back from the front of the column. "Shep and Aniceto will help us keep out of any prairie dog towns along the way."

Though nightfall robbed them of visibility, the cool made for easier going. They posted along at a medium trot, with intermittent pauses as Aniceto made sure they were still following the sign. They went along this way until almost ten o'clock, when the halt called by Aniceto lasted much longer than the previous interludes.

"Do you reckon he's lost the trail?" Wiswall said, leaning on his saddle horn as they waited for the call to resume.

"Can't tell," Andrews said. "But if he can't find it, it's sure as hell none of us can, either."

Baylor called the men together. "Aniceto says that the Apaches went up there." He pointed east, toward the nearby outcroppings that mounted up the sides of the Sierra Diablos. "Harder to trail them. But the cavalry is still headed north. We'll continue trailing them until we get to where the troops are."

"I imagine they'll be somewhere around Rattlesnake Spring, judging from the line of travel," Gillett said. "I'd guess we're about . . . thirty-five miles out?" He looked at Aniceto for confirmation and received a nod.

"All right, then. We've got our destination," Baylor said. "Let's mount up. And don't nod off."

"Not much damned chance of that," one of the men mumbled.

Chapter 4

At about midnight, the saddle-weary, bleary-eyed Rangers caught up to the Tenth Cavalry's supply train: two mule-drawn ambulances and a freight wagon, guarded by more than a dozen heavily armed outriders. They soon discovered that Colonel Grierson himself was riding in the freight wagon, which was being driven by his son.

"Good evening, Colonel," Baylor said, drawing up beside the wagon. "A little late for an excursion, wouldn't you say? And not much moonlight to illuminate the view."

The colonel gave a low chuckle. "Good to see you, Lieutenant Baylor. I take it you deduced that Victorio bypassed Eagle Spring, and that we followed him?"

"We did, sir."

"Very well. May I suggest that you and your men ride on ahead to Rattlesnake Spring, where I believe you will find most of my command, along with elements of the Twenty-fourth Infantry, established there and eagerly awaiting the arrival of our guest of honor."

"We gather he took to the hills to cover his tracks."

"Yes. But what he gains in stealth, he loses in speed. My men left Eagle Spring yesterday evening and rode all night to arrive in time to arrange a proper welcome for Victorio."

"Impressive, sir."

"We'll be glad to have your Rangers alongside us when the festivities begin."

"In that case, Colonel, we'll be on our way. Good luck and safe journey to you."

"And the same to you, Lieutenant."

About an hour later, the Ranger column jogged into the broad valley that separated the Sierra Diablos on the west from the Delaware and Apache Mountains on the east. They found matters just as Colonel Grierson had described: in the canyon passes and other approaches to the spring, Captain Viele had deployed the Buffalo Soldiers of Companies C and G of the Tenth Cavalry.

"The colonel's strategy is to deny Victorio the canyon passes and watering holes," Viele explained to Baylor as the Rangers dismounted. "We've got forces stationed all through the Trans-Pecos, watching for him. But we think he'll come through here, probably making for the Guadalupes. He'll find us well prepared."

The Rangers watered their mounts before deploying along the rim of one of the nearby passes. "Sergeant Gillett, check with the cavalry officer of the watch and see how we need to fill in the roster," Baylor said. "Otherwise, boys, get a little rest. If Victorio stays true to form, we won't see any action before daylight."

"I don't believe I need a second invitation," Wiswall said, tugging the saddle off his mare and scraping the lather from her back with the saddle blanket. "I might fall asleep, leaning against Mousey, here."

"I'll find a little something for Shep to eat," Andrews said, "and then I will gladly follow your example."

The night passed quietly, its only interruption

coming when, about half past three in the morning, Colonel Grierson rolled into camp, with the freight wagon, the ambulances, and his mounted escort. Wiswall roused just enough to hear the low murmur of the voices as the colonel conferred with Captain Viele, but he settled his head back against the seat of his saddle and was soon unconscious again.

The ponies picked their way carefully along the shoulders of the canyons, the warriors careful to keep their line of travel far enough below the ridgelines that they did not risk revealing themselves to any who might be watching from a distance.

Victorio's eyes ceaselessly roamed the rocky slopes, dotted with yucca and lechuguilla. Now and then, one of the men slid down from his pony and sliced some of the fleshy leaves from the base of a lechuguilla plant. He would gash it lengthwise with his knife and suck the moisture as it oozed through the cut. The warriors could sustain themselves in this way, even in the heat of the day, but it was insufficient for the ponies. They needed to reach the water at Rattlesnake Spring.

The previous spring, before the summer's heat had clamped its brazen grip on the land, Victorio's band had been living in a good camp in the Hembrillo country, not far north of here. There was plenty of water from two springs, and the surrounding Guadalupe Mountains provided ample concealment for the people.

But one day, near sundown, two formations of bluecoats with dark skin, the tireless ones with the wooly hair his people called Buffalo Soldiers, approached the draw that held the precious springs. It was too late for concealment; the soldiers' scouts had already seen the signs of the people's use of the place. The bluecoats became wary; they shouldered their guns as they moved toward the springs.

Victorio had held his braves back until the last moment. They had crouched behind boulders along the canyon rims and ridges, watching in silence as the dark-faced bluecoats wound along the pass from the northwest, getting closer and closer to the point where Victorio and his people would have no choice but to wipe them out in order to avoid losing their safe hiding place.

He had given the signal: a screech like that of the red-tailed hawk on a warm summer updraft. His warriors had fired their guns and released their arrows down at the bluecoats. Two of them fell and were quickly dragged behind rocks by their comrades. Many of the horses and mules fell screaming, with blood spouting from their necks and arrows sunk into their vitals.

The bluecoats were pinned down below Victorio and his people, but they formed skirmish lines and took cover behind the ridges below the heights occupied by the Apaches. Victorio's warriors could not rush down to engage them, for they were armed with the deadly accurate Winchester and Springfield carbines favored by the bluecoats; if his fighters showed themselves carelessly, they would fall with a bullet in their chests.

Night came down, and in the darkness, the Apaches began cautiously encroaching upon the bluecoats' position. By the time the sky was turning pink over the Guadalupe peaks in the east, they were almost ready to mount their final attack.

But then, more bluecoats came pouring into the passes from the north and the west. Among them were Apache scouts from the traitor tribes who helped the bluecoats to fight and kill their own people. And there were more of the Buffalo Soldiers and the whites, mounted on fresh horses and heavily armed.

Victorio and his warriors had no choice but to fall back to the peak above the south spring, to cover the flight of the women and children. The aging Nana led them away from the camp, through the ravines and canyons, south toward the big river and Mexico, while Victorio and his warriors fought a rearguard action to keep the bluecoats at bay.

In the end, they had to surrender their camp when, still heavily engaged by the bluecoats slowly forcing their way up the slopes toward Victorio, they realized they were being flanked from the west by a detachment of the Indian scouts. Victorio and his warriors had fled to the north and west, trying to draw the bluecoats away from Nana and the escaping women and children. Their camp was destroyed, and they left three warriors dead on the battlefield.

Since then, Victorio and his people had been going back and forth, crossing and re-crossing the Rio Grande, trying to find a place where they could breathe, where they could rest. They were growing weary. Victorio did not know how much longer they would be able to stay ahead of the bluecoats, the far-roving Rangers, and the brown-coated militias to the south of the Rio Grande. Sometimes his fighters would capture a stagecoach as it wound along the roads through the canyons near the river; they would drive the mules back to the camp, where they could provide meat for a few days. Sometimes they could take cattle from an isolated rancho. So far, they had been able either to kill or elude those who came after them.

But the bluecoats would not give up. The Buffalo Soldiers were tireless riders and hard fighters; the Rangers, though they went in small bands, traveled light and fast. And all of them were better armed than Victorio's people. They had the repeating Winchesters and the Springfields; they had the dreaded Sharps that could kill a man from a mile away.

One day, there would be a fight that Victorio would not be able to flee—a last fight, when the light would go out of his eyes and his enemy would stand over his lifeless body. He did not know when that fight would come, but each day it felt closer. And then, who would protect the women and children? Who would teach the old stories to the young ones?

Riding slowly along the flinty ridge, Victorio remembered the day, back in the winter, when he had talked to the white-eye outside the abandoned stagecoach station at Crow Spring. He remembered the dog, and how the man said that he was willing to die to save its life. He had allowed the white man and the Rangers with him to go free. He had let them go back to their station at Ysleta, taking their guns and their dog with them.

Victorio was still not sure why he had allowed them to live that day. Was it the faithfulness of the dog? Could such a good animal give its loyalty to a man with a black heart? Victorio was not sure. Maybe the man whose life he had spared that day would be the same man who would kill him. Maybe the dog would sniff his corpse as his master wiped Victorio's blood from his knife.

Where are you now, brother of coyote? Are you help-
ing your master to track me? Will you bring the bluecoats
and their guns to kill my people?

Suddenly, Victorio's head snapped up. What was

it? Something was wrong. He pulled his pony to a stop and held up an arm. As one, his braves halted, sitting their mounts as still as stones, nothing moving except their eyes, scouring the hillsides and crags for any sign of trouble.

They were about to enter the pass that would lead them to the spring. Victorio could smell the water, and the ponies could, too. They yearned to go forward, to quench their long thirst from the rough trek through the broken slopes of the Sierra Diablo. But every fiber in Victorio's body told him that to enter that pass was death. Though nothing moved and there was no sound except the sighing of the wind, he knew his enemies were nearby, waiting for him to ride into their gunsights.

"Turn around," he said. "We cannot—"

A bullet splintered a rock on the slope, just past his head. He crouched low and wheeled his pony around. With a war cry, he kicked his pony forward to the nearest rock outcropping. He dove behind it and swatted the horse's flank to make it keep running, out of the reach of the attacking bluecoats and their guns. His warriors scattered for cover. In front of Victorio, down the slope toward the canyon floor, one of the ponies lay on its side, kicking and screaming in pain as its blood gushed onto the rocky ground. Some part of Victorio's mind realized that this was Kaytennae's mount. He hoped Kaytennae was not dead.

He unslung his battered Enfield rifle and peered around the edge of a boulder, trying to find out where the gunfire was coming from, trying to find an enemy to kill.

Chapter 5

"They've fallen back," Captain Viele called. "Hold your fire, unless you've got a target you can hit."

Andrews jacked a .50-caliber cartridge into the breech of his rifle and peered cautiously around the lower edge of the boulder. Unlike the Buffalo Soldiers of the Tenth, who mostly carried Winchesters, he had a Sharps. Its thirty-four-inch barrel gave him an accurate range of up to a thousand yards. If he could bring down one of the Apaches from far away, it might give the others pause before trying to rush the Ranger and army positions.

He heard the voices of the Apaches, bouncing off the canyon walls as they shouted back and forth. But he couldn't see anything except the horse he had brought down with his first shot. Its movements were slowing; the pool of blood in which it lay had spread. The rider had fallen off, and at first Andrews had thought he had taken down one of the warriors, but he had clearly escaped and was now crouched in some hidden fold of the rough terrain.

The Apaches' voices quieted, and Andrews, with the others, watched nervously, their fingers curled over the triggers of their weapons. It was mid-afternoon, and the August sun bore down on the rocky slopes and the canyon floor. Andrews could feel his clothes sticking to his back, his legs. He tugged down his hat brim against the glare, trying not to blink any more than necessary.

What had made Victorio pause? Since barely after sunrise, Andrews and the others had been hunkered down around the spring and the high places in the passes leading to it, waiting in silence to spring their ambush. The only noise all morning had been the sound of the hot, dry wind, sliding along the ravines like a draft from Lucifer's own oven. All morning and past midday they had lain in wait, baking in their own juices.

Somewhere over the shoulder of the slope to his right, Andrews heard Shep start barking. At that same instant, a volley of gunfire and arrows erupted from his left, as some thirty Apaches charged out of a ravine toward the spring and the ten or fifteen Buffalo Soldiers who were dug in there.

Andrews swung around and opened fire, as did the riflemen stationed all around him on the hillside. The Apache assault broke in half, then faltered as the storm of gunfire from above and in front of them blunted their momentum. They scattered for such cover as they could find. Andrews saw a brave dragging one of his fellows whose legs seemed no longer to support his weight.

Another wave of Apaches charged from a different quarter, supported by heavy fire from the first attackers, shooting from their concealed positions. The cavalrymen met this new threat with a return volley, and at that moment, Companies B and H of the Tenth charged into the ravine on horseback from two different directions, intent upon riding down the Indians who were attempting to rush the spring.

Seeing that they were badly outnumbered and out-maneuvered, the Apaches broke off the attack, falling back to protected positions along the sides of the canyons. The engagement became a matter of occasional exchanges of fire between the opposing forces, both dug into their positions. Andrews scoured the hillsides and ravines for another target, but the Apaches kept themselves well hidden.

An hour and a half crept by under the pitiless glare of the sun. Then Andrews heard the sound of hoofbeats and wagon wheels coming from the southeast.

"That there be Captain Gilmore and the resupply train from Fort Davis," Andrews heard someone say nearby. "Hope they kept they powder dry."

A sarcastic response about the likelihood of enough moisture to spoil the ammunition came to Andrews's mind, but before he could verbalize it, they heard gunfire coming from the same direction as the approaching wagons. Not long after that, the Apache fighters hidden in the arroyo charged once more, this time apparently making for the pack mules picketed behind the defensive lines near the spring. Once again, a hail of bullets from the Buffalo Soldiers and Rangers defending the springs halted the assault, and the Apaches melted back into the shelter of the rocks and ravines.

After maybe five minutes of tense waiting, they heard a sound peal out across the canyons: the cry of a hawk. But there was no hawk in the sky.

"What do you calculate that means?" Andrews said, to no one in particular.

"I expects we gonna have to wait and find out," said the man just down the slope. "Keep a sharp lookout."

The afternoon wore down toward evening. Andrews felt like bacon too long on the griddle, but he dared not move nor allow his eyes to cease their wary roving across the broken terrain.

As shadows lengthened across the baking hillsides and canyon floors, the Apaches tried three more times to force their way to the spring. Each time, the superior fire of the defenders drove them back, dragging their wounded. The final attempt came as the last of the daylight faded, and it ended with Victorio's fighters falling back from the positions they had held all afternoon, in full retreat.

"After them, boys!" Captain Viele shouted; the bugler blew "Advance" for all he was worth. With those all around him, Andrews sprang up and ran down the flinty slope as fast as he could, trying to overtake their fleeing enemies.

As they reached the low-lying area around the spring, some thirty mounted Buffalo Soldiers thundered past. As Andrews and the others watched, the riders vanished among the ravines. For several minutes, they heard intermittent shouts and the occasional report of a firearm, each time seeming to come from a greater distance.

They found the bodies of four of Victorio's men, left behind by their retreating comrades. When they assembled back at the spring, the roll call revealed that one of the privates of Company C, a man named Wesley Hardy, was unaccounted for. All of Baylor's Rangers were present.

Andrews walked over to Wiswall; Shep was standing beside him. "Well, I see you two are none the worse for wear."

"He stayed at my side the whole time," Wiswall said. "I nearly jumped out of my skin when he started barking, right before the first onslaught. I guess he was trying to warn us."

Andrews nodded. "Most likely so. Must have smelled or heard something."

Wiswall peered away, toward the ravines where the mounted patrol had disappeared. "None of the four dead were Victorio. I guess he'll live to fight another day."

"Unless they run him down."

Wiswall shook his head. "Not a lot of light left; I don't much think they'll find him tonight."

"If he can see an ambush before he rides into it, I calculate he can avoid troopers in the dark," Andrews said.

"But even the Apaches can't hide from thirst," Sergeant Gillett said, kneeling down to pet Shep. "If the army can keep him from the waterholes, the desert will do the rest. And as long as we've got this old fellow here with us, we'll be all right." He smiled as he scratched Shep behind the ears. "He's our good luck charm."

"There were more of them than we thought," Kaytennae said, balancing precariously on the hindquarters of the pony that now carried him, along with Victorio, as it picked its way along, head down in the dark.

"I think they are guarding the water against us," Victorio said. "They know they can never catch us in the open country, but the water does not move. And they are many—their guns are many."

"Our ponies must have water."

"There is no water for us on this side of the big river," Victorio said. "We must go back to Mexico. We will ride the ponies as far as they can take us, and if they die under us, we will walk the rest of the way. There is no other choice."

They rode for a while in silence, and Victorio tried

to decide on a plan. He hoped that one of the runners he had sent to the supply camp in the Sierra Diablos would arrive in time to warn them, to save the few cattle and spare horses remaining to the band.

"The dog is still with them," Kaytennae said. "He told them when we were about to attack."

Victorio nodded. "I have been thinking about that, Kaytennae. I am not so sure he was trying to warn the whites and the dark-skinned ones."

"What else is possible? He heard our approach. He scented us, maybe. And he barked, to tell them we were coming."

"Maybe. Or maybe he was trying to warn us. Maybe his spirit was whispering to me when we approached; maybe that is why we stopped before we rode into their gun sights. Maybe when he barked, he was trying to tell us to turn back—that there were too many of them to fight."

"I wish we had stopped sooner. Four of our braves will see no more sunrises."

"If we had kept going, our losses would have been far greater," Victorio said.

"On the day Itza-chu saw him," Kaytennae said a while later, "when you sent him to the place of the Rangers near Ysleta, he told me that he said to the dog, 'May we never meet in anger, brother of Coyote.' Maybe what you say is true; maybe he is trying to keep us out of a fight we cannot win."

In the darkness, Victorio smiled. "You can ask him yourself, Kaytennae."

"What does that mean?"

"The brother of Coyote will come again. You will see."

Chapter 6

The wheels of the stagecoach raised thin trails of dust into the hot, still air as it came toward the canyon. From his position among the rocks at the top of the canyon rim, Victorio watched his braves below, waiting like coiled cougars as the stagecoach approached their hiding place.

They needed replacements for their fatigued and failing ponies, and the two little Spanish mules pulling the wagon would be a help. The passengers and driver might have weapons or other supplies they could use. The old fort, recently re-occupied by the bluecoats, was only a few miles distant, but Victorio was hoping that they could strike quickly, take the mules and any other valuables, and be across the river into Mexico before the army had time to mount a pursuit.

Victorio had selected the ten or twelve freshest mounts and put his best riders on them. They went down to the canyon and positioned themselves just on the far side of a tight turn in the trail, to keep from being seen for as long as possible. He watched as the stagecoach came nearer and nearer to the bend in the trail. He could hear the sound of the harness chains and the mules' hoof beats, the shouting of the driver.

The stagecoach rounded the bend in the trail, and Victorio's braves fired almost immediately; he saw the puffs of smoke from their guns and, an instant later, heard the loud reports that echoed along the canyon wall. The driver hauled the team around. Somehow, he got the mules turned back in the direction he had come and was plying his whip and shouting even louder.

As Victorio watched, his warriors gave chase, trying to get ahead of the stagecoach and grab the leads of the running mules. But the canyon was narrow, and the tough little mules were fresh and scared. The riders could not get past the stagecoach. Soon they would be out of the canyon and into the open country leading to the fort; they would not be able to catch the coach in time.

Victorio could see a man's head and arm hanging out of the window of the stagecoach—a passenger, he guessed. From the way the figure flopped bonelessly as the stagecoach rolled over the rough trail, the man was either dead or badly wounded.

As Victorio had instructed them, his riders pulled up at the opening of the canyon. The ponies were just too tired—and the driver of the stagecoach too lucky.

Victorio began walking toward his horse. "We ride south now," he said over his shoulder to the young brave who waited with him. "Tell the others."

Aniceto picked his way down the slope to the ravine where the troop waited, holding their horses by the bits. "What have you found?" Baylor said, as the other Rangers gathered close.

"Five men, six horses, two mules, and twenty or thirty head of cattle," the Tigua scout said in a low voice. "Many riders left here, two, maybe three days ago, going north."

"The bunch we fought at Rattlesnake Spring, I'd wager," Sergeant Gillett said.

"This is Victorio's supply camp," Baylor said. "We need to send word to the cavalry." He turned to the other men. "Where were they when we last heard from him?"

"A detachment of the Tenth was just west of here, headed south," George Lloyd said. "I saw their dust earlier this morning."

"Ride over and find them," Baylor said. "Take a couple of men with you. We'll keep an eye on things here until we get some help."

"I'll go, Lieutenant," Andrews said.

"I guess somebody had better go along to keep an eye on you," Wiswall said. He swung into his saddle, and Shep, who had been lying in the shade of a boulder, stood up and padded over to Wiswall's horse. "Looks like Shep is coming, too," Wiswall said.

Andrews, Wiswall, and Lloyd were soon headed across the scrubland that lay between the Sierra Diablos and the Carrizo Mountains, lying to the west. They had been riding for maybe half an hour, at an easy canter, when they picked up the dust rising from a mounted column, headed southeast along the eastern edge of the Carrizos.

"That'll be them," Lloyd said. They pressed their mounts into a gallop and bore down on the cavalry detachment, drawing within hailing distance about fifteen minutes later.

It was Troop A of the Tenth Cavalry, led by Captain Nolan. The three Rangers rode to the front of the halted column. At Nolan's right hand was Lieutenant Flipper, the first black man to graduate from West Point and the one responsible for notifying Colonel Grierson of Victorio's latest entrance into Texas.

"Captain Nolan, our scout has led us to what we believe is Victorio's supply camp," Lloyd said. "There's quite a few head of livestock there, and we thought the cavalry would want to know."

"Thank you, Ranger," the captain said. He turned to his second-in-command. "Lieutenant Flipper, take ten men and go back with these Rangers. When you've secured the livestock and dealt with any hostiles you may encounter, proceed to Fort Quitman, where we'll brief the colonel."

Flipper gave a smart salute and wheeled his horse around. He motioned quickly to ten of the mounted Buffalo Soldiers, and soon they were headed back to the east, following Andrews, Wiswall, Lloyd, and Shep, hurrying back to rejoin their companions.

As they were nearing the ravine where they had left Baylor and the others, gunshots sounded from over the crest of the ravine, in the direction of the Apache camp. They pressed their mounts into a full gallop and armed themselves.

Pounding down the ravine and rounding its shoulder, they came upon a scene of pandemonium: Rangers were firing down into the camp as cattle bawled and swirled and unmounted horses shied this way and that. A handful of Apaches were running for the rocks on the east side of the camp, firing rifles at the attacking Rangers as they went.

Andrews, Wiswall, and Lloyd vaulted from their saddles and hunkered down behind the nearest cover, each of them trying simultaneously to assess the situation and draw a bead on an enemy combatant. Wiswall heard Lieutenant Flipper shouting something to the men in his command, and he heard the sound of horses whinnying and their shod hooves clattering on the rocks as they wheeled and raced away in another direction.

The panicked livestock made it difficult to see what was going on. Ranger Lloyd leaned over to Wiswall and shouted, "Grab your horse, if you can, and let's keep the horses and cattle from getting out of this little swale here. Maybe we can keep them bunched up against that rock wall, yonder."

Miraculously, Wiswall's mount hadn't gone far and he was able to gather the reins and swing into the saddle. He leaned down toward Shep and pointed at the distressed beasts. "Let's keep them here, Shep." Seeing a brace of Apache ponies headed toward the mouth of the canyon, Wiswall started on a course to head them off, with Shep sprinting ahead, barking.

After a while, with the aid of some of the other Rangers, they were able to contain most of the captured animals in the low place among the ridges where the Apaches had been camping.

"We'll drive these animals to Fort Quitman," Baylor announced, as the dust started to settle. "They won't be of any further use to Victorio. They were likely stolen from some rancho or other, as the band was on its way here."

In another hour, Lieutenant Flipper and his detail came back.

"Did you catch them?" Baylor asked.

Flipper shook his head. "I'm afraid not, Lieutenant. They slipped away among the breaks. Best we can tell, though, they're still afoot. We may be able to pick them up as they try to make their way back to the Rio Grande."

As the men gathered up and Sergeant Gillett assigned various Rangers to herd duty, Baylor related to Andrews, Wiswall, and Lloyd what had taken place after they left to summon the cavalry.

"Most of us were gathered up in the ravine. I sent Aniceto and two other men back up into the rocks to keep an eye on the camp while we waited for reinforcement.

"Then, in a while, we heard ponies coming along the ridge. Next thing we knew, the Apaches were yelling and running among the livestock. It looked to Aniceto like some braves had come along, likely from the scrape up north, and told the men guarding the camp what had happened. They were about to break camp and head for the river when Aniceto and the others yelled down at us. We ran up to the top of the ridge, and that was when the fireworks started."

"How far are we from Quitman?" Andrews asked.

"We'll come around the southern foot of the Carrizos, then we'll strike the mail road. I imagine it's a good eight hours, anyway, pushing this livestock."

Wiswall peered up at the sun. "We might make it before dark."

Baylor nodded. "Best we get started, though."

Victorio watched as the young men took the lifeless body of the herdsman and shoved it, head-first, into the scalding pot of tallow. They laughed as the flesh of the corpse crackled, then wrinkled their noses and said bad words about the smell of the burning hair.

Victorio wondered, as he watched, how many of these young men would still be alive by winter. The bluecoats, the Rangers, and the Mexican militia came closer and closer to victory each time they met. Each scalp his fighters took, each act of ritual torture, each enemy killed by arrow, bullet, or knife added one more reason why they would receive no mercy when the inevitable defeat finally came.

But he did nothing to stop them. They were humiliating their enemies, as victorious Apaches had done for generations. They were fighters, warriors, sons of the wolf. This was all that was left to them—for a little while. They would die by their enemies' hands, but at least they would die as free men. Maybe that was enough.

"Drive the cattle toward the river," Victorio said. "Take the fresh horses. We must go now; the bluecoats will be coming."

Chapter 7

Victorio led his war party toward the big mountain that overlooked the main road from the city of Chihuahua to the town the whites called El Paso del Norte. They moved the cattle along the dry, dusty plains toward the mountain, easily distinguished by its distinctive peak, resembling a stump of wax candle: the Mexicans called it Cerro Candelaria—"Candle Hill."

But it was much more than a hill. Its peak commanded a view of some thirty miles in every direction. From such a vantage point, Victorio and his people would have long advance warning of any approaching force.

Almost a year before, this view had served them well, had enabled them to teach the Mexicans a lesson. Through a spy, Victorio had word that the people of Carrizal intended to lure him into a trap; they would pretend to be friendly and then, at the right time, they would treacherously turn and kill him and his people. In return, their government would give them a bounty for Apache scalps. Sure enough, before too many days had passed, a small group came out from the town, carrying a white flag of truce and inviting Victorio and his people to a fiesta.

In the past, Victorio had been able to trade horses and cattle to these people for guns and ammunition. But now, they wanted to kill him for money. Victorio had to show the people of Carrizal that he was not to be trifled with. He laid a plan, and then he sent a small raiding band to steal some horses from a rancho on the outskirts of Carrizal.

When men from Carrizal came looking for the horses, Victorio's watchers atop Candelaria had seen them coming from a long way off. They had plenty of time to prepare a trap for the Mexicans, and none of them lived to return to their village. And then, a few days later, when a larger party came to find out why the men had not returned, Victorio and his braves had carried out the same strategy a second time. When the Mexicans sent out a big war party, led by the Rangers from Ysleta, their approach was plain for long before they drew near, and it was a simple matter to move the people into hiding until the intruders had tended to their dead and dispersed back to their homes. After that, no more Mexicans came to bother them for a long time in their camp in the hills.

These cattle they had just taken from the rancho across the river would buy Victorio's people precious time to rest. They could stay in the broken country, away from the eyes of the *milicianos* and the hacendados. They could slaughter some of the cattle and dry the meat to carry on long rides and to provide food through the long winter when hunting was poor. They could use the hides to repair their tools and clothing.

Victorio thought about the times when he was still a boy, when the Chihenne still lived in the lands of their ancestors, to the north, in the place the whites called New Mexico. In the forested mountains there had always been deer and elk. In the grasslands and the valleys of the Mimbres River, Victorio and his people could always find wild turkey, pronghorns, and even buffalo, in the days before the whites with the far-shooting rifles hunted them into nonexistence. They could take silvery trout and darting bream from the clear streams. The air under the pines was clean and cool. The Chihenne had lived there as they were intended to live—as Usen had created the *nideh* to live.

Victorio remembered the day when, as a young man, he had first ridden the trail south with Nana, into Mexico. The whites and Mexicans were pushing farther and farther into the lands of the Chihenne and the other tribes. That was when the Mexicans had first placed a bounty on their heads; a chief of the people was slain in a massacre near the place close to the headwaters of the Mimbres River where the whites took copper ore from the side of a mountain. War had come.

Nana was a wise leader, and Geronimo, one of his war chiefs, was fearless. They took horses and cattle from northern Mexico and struck fear into the hearts of many of their enemies. And then, when the big war between the whites came a few years later, Victorio had followed Dasoda-hae, whom the Mexicans named Mangas Coloradas—"Red Sleeves"—because of all the blood he spilled from his enemies. During that time, while the whites were killing each other far to the east, the Chihenne, the Mescalero, and the Chiricahua had moved throughout New Mexico, Texas, and northern Mexico almost as they pleased.

But the bluecoats returned. And when Mangas Coloradas had tried to talk peace with them, he was slain by treachery: taken under a flag of truce and killed like a dog. They even chopped off his head and sent it east in a box, a curiosity for their medicine men.

Someone was coming toward them. As Victorio watched, one of his young men rode out to meet the one who approached. As they came closer, Victorio recognized Taklishim, one of the old men who had gone south with Nana, before the fight at Rattlesnake Spring.

"Nana has moved the camp farther north, toward the slopes of the Corralitos," the older man said when he neared Victorio. "The water is better there."

Victorio nodded. "It is good. Go back and tell him we have cattle. Take one of the young men with you."

"You have used up your entire lifetime of luck, I judge," Sergeant Gillett said, shaking his head as he studied the stagecoach. "There's scarcely a square inch on this wagon of yours that doesn't sport a bullet hole, a groove where a bullet grazed it, or a gouge from an arrowhead."

"Three of the spokes are shot in two," Andrews said, pointing. "Hard to imagine how the rims didn't collapse."

"Well, sir, I reckon the good Lord just didn't want them redskins to take me," Ed Walde said. "I guarantee you, I was laying the leather to them mules like the devil his own self was chasing me."

"Not far off," Gillett said. "Poor old General Byrne would say the same, if he could."

"Speaking of which," Wiswall said, looking up from the ruined stagecoach, "it looks like they're about ready to start the festivities."

The four men, with Shep trailing them, walked over to the porch of the command post. On their shoulders, six of the Buffalo Soldiers supported the simple wooden box that contained the earthly remains of General

James J. Byrne, an official of the Texas and Pacific Railway. Led by Lieutenant Baylor, the Rangers and some of the men from Company K of the Tenth formed up in double file behind the coffin and made a quiet procession to a place on a rocky hillside just past the corrals of Fort Quitman. A shallow grave waited there.

The pallbearers lowered the coffin onto two ropes placed parallel on the ground beside the freshly dug grave. Taking up the ends of the ropes, they raised the coffin and lowered it slowly into the ground. Forming a loose circle around the gravesite, the men all removed their hats.

Captain Nolan, the commander of Company K, cleared his throat and offered a brief prayer. Lieutenant Baylor read the Twenty-third Psalm from the battered Bible he carried in his saddlebag.

Captain Nolan turned and nodded at the rifle squad who stood in a line, five yards away. The corporal gave the terse commands, and the soldiers shouldered their weapons in unison, then fired a volley up and over the heads of those gathered around the grave. The sound of the reports echoed away among the rocky hillsides.

The men put their hats back on and walked slowly back toward the command post, except for the Buffalo Soldiers on the burial detail, who began filling in the grave with flinty soil and rocks.

"Well, it's a damned shame the general happened to be traveling on the same day that Victorio and his bunch were headed for the Mexican side of the river," Andrews said. "Too bad he didn't get a little dose of your luck, Walde—just enough to keep him alive, anyhow."

"Well, he weren't killed outright," Walde said. "I could hear him a-groaning, over the racket the wagon and mules were making. But when they shot at the coach, a bullet caught him in the thigh, and one in the chest. They done all they could for him here at the fort, but the wounds turned septic, and I reckon that's what finally killed him."

"One more sin to lay to Victorio's charge, I suppose," Andrews said.

"I'm powerful sorry about it," Walde said. "In fact, I was kind of hoping I could talk to Sergeant Gillett to see if he might be willing to put in a word for me with Lieutenant Baylor, so I could join up with you Rangers and help bring Victorio to justice."

"I'll say something to the sergeant for you," Wiswall said. "I'm sure he will appreciate the offer."

"Least I can do," the stage driver said.

"I heard Lieutenant Baylor say they picked up the trail of the Apaches just east of here—where they ambushed the stage, I guess," Andrews said.

"They're surely well into Mexico by now," Wiswall said.

"I calculate that's right. I guess our Indian chasing is done for a while, unless he crosses back into Texas," Andrews said.

"Well, I'd sure like a chance to even the score with that old red devil," Walde said.

"I wouldn't worry about it," Wiswall said. "I've got a feeling we haven't seen or heard the last of him." He looked down at Shep. "What do you say, old boy? Are we going to meet up with Victorio again, any time soon?"

The dog stared intently at Wiswall for several seconds.

"You reckon that means 'yes'?" Andrews said.

Wiswall smiled and slowly shook his head. "Why are you asking me? I'm not smart enough to know what this damned dog is thinking."

Chapter 8

Nana shifted his bad leg. He made no sound, but Victorio saw the old chief's eyes twitch with pain.

"We must go west, Bidu-ya," the old man said. "To Juh and his people in the Blue Mountains. There is no other way."

"You may be right," Victorio said. "And yet, my heart still hopes for Ojo Caliente, for the Mimbres country . . . for the Cañada Alamosa and the place that Usen made for the stewardship of our people. Maybe the whites will still listen to me. Maybe one of my messengers will get through to them with words that they can understand."

"The whites understand your words, Bidu-ya. But it does not matter. They will never willingly let the Chihenne back in the Cañada Alamosa. Their people now graze their cattle in the draws between the mountains. They dig for copper and iron ore in the sides of the hills. They will not allow the Chihenne to return.

"And their fighters grow stronger and smarter. They have learned the lesson you taught the bluecoat Morrow when he followed you into Mexico; they guard the water on the north side of the big river against us. Their Rangers ride the border, and their bluecoats dog our steps wherever we turn. Your warriors have spilled their blood. They will never make peace."

"But what of Cochise, Nana? He fought the Mexicans and the bluecoats for many years, yet he was able to make a treaty with them."

"The bluecoats were weary from fighting each other, back in the east," Nana said. "And besides, that treaty died with Cochise." The old man idly poked a stick at the small blaze that flickered at his feet. "Neither of his sons are the man that Cochise was. The Chiricahua will have no more peace from the whites."

"I would be content if I could make a treaty with the whites that would last until my death," Victorio said. "I am tired of watching the women and children suffer in the sun of summer, with no cool stream or spring nearby. I am weary from thinking about how many of our people are still trapped in that place of heat and sickness on the San Carlos reservation. For too long the Chihenne have had to remain on the move, always avoiding enemies. There has been no time to properly teach the young ones the ways of our people. The new mothers have no old men to carve the *tsoch* for their babies to lie in—all the old men are dead."

"All except me," Nana said with his lopsided smile. "And maybe a couple of others."

Victorio stared into the tiny fire. Somewhere in a ravine behind him, one of the ponies nickered softly. Farther away, a cougar sent a hunting scream up into the night air.

"It is good that you brought the cattle," Nana said. "The Rangers found the others, the men said. And the horses. They had to walk back. Only three of the five braves returned."

Victorio shook his head. "We have lost too many

fighters. And still we are thirsty and tired." He looked up at Nana. "Who fell?"

"Aska-do-dilges and Goyathlay."

"Both the sons of Maa-ya-ha."

Nana nodded. "She was too tired to wail for them when she got the news. And too thirsty to weep."

"Some of the cattle became mired when we crossed the big river," Victorio said, after a minute or two had passed. "The men were so hungry that they cut pieces of flesh from the living beasts. They could not stand for the whole animal to fall to the bluecoats who chased us."

"If we are to make the journey to Juh, we will need even more meat for drying," Nana said. "And too many of the people are now on foot."

Victorio looked into the depths of the coals from the small fire. They glowed, now bright, now dark, like something breathing. "The rancho of Don Mariano Samaniego-Delgado is not too far. We can find horses and cattle there."

"He is a friend of the provincial governor," Nana said. "He has the ears of the commanders of the *milicianos*." He looked at Victorio for a long time. "Will he not seek revenge?"

"We must have meat and mounts," Victorio said in a sharp tone. "You said it yourself, Nana. We do not have time to trade—and nothing to trade anyway, except dust and bones."

The old chief nodded, studying the small, licking tongues of flame, becoming smaller and smaller as the greasewood sticks were consumed. After a while, he said, "It is a long way to the Blue Mountains. And little water along the way."

"We need ammunition, also," Victorio said. "We cannot fight the bluecoats with arrows and knives."

"I know where to trade for ammunition," Nana said, "or where to take it."

"You are too valuable," Victorio said quickly. "Send three or four of your smartest young men. But do not leave the people. They need you."

Nana nodded. He gave a sad smile. "There was a time when I would have fought you, right here and right now, just to show you that I was a warrior of the Chihenne, and no man alive—you included—could tell me to stay with the old men and the women while others go out to do deeds of courage. But now . . . I think that you are right, Bidu-ya. I will send out some young men."

The flames were now barely a purple shadow, hovering over the remaining coals. After a while, Victorio said, "It is better to do it soon, Nana, so that we will have ready weapons for the journey."

"It is always necessary to have ready weapons."

"I will send out some men to look at the Samaniego rancho," Victorio said. "I will talk to them tomorrow. We will start getting ready to make our move. Still, I hope that the whites will finally listen."

"It is good to hope," Nana said, after a long time. "But it is also good to be ready."

The raiders crept to the top of the rocky outcropping and carefully peered over. The main herd was below them on the grassy flat that spread on either side of the small, winding creek. Mesquite and cenizo dotted the landscape where the horses and mules grazed.

Kaytennae signed to the others to spread out and make sure they knew where the herdsmen were stationed. Don Mariano usually sent no fewer than four vaqueros out with his herds, and so far they had only been able to put eyes on two mounted men. Both of them had been carrying modern Winchester carbines, which made it even more important for the Apaches to know where they were, since they were already at a disadvantage in arms. An undetected vaquero with good aim could disrupt their plan, with disastrous and deadly consequences.

After a while, Kaytennae heard the call of a white-winged dove, far to his right. That meant that one of his men had located one of Don Samaniego's riders. After he had lain in the hot sun for another space of time, a similar call came from his right. The horses had not betrayed any nervousness, so they had probably not been detected. It was time to put their plan into motion.

After a final long look at the herd and the lay of the land, Kaytennae worked his way back down the slope and went to rejoin his men in the arroyo where the boy waited with their ponies. On the way, he used his belt knife to shear off a leaf of lechuguilla, sucking the moisture from it as he walked. It was hot. They needed to get the horses started and put some distance between themselves and the ranch, then find water for their ponies and the new horses. Victorio would be counting on them to bring the horses in good shape, ready to bear the Chihenne to a place of safety, far from the bluecoats and the Mexicans.

Using hand motions and only as many low-voiced words as necessary, Kaytennae made sure his men understood what was to happen next. They checked their weapons and ammunition, then vaulted onto their ponies. The four of them rode out of the arroyo and separated.

Kaytennae reached his hiding place in a small

thicket of mesquite that gave him a view of the herd. When he judged that the rest of his men were in place, he gave the signal: the cry of a red-tailed hawk. He kicked his pony and charged from the thicket, bearing down on the nearest animals in the herd at a full gallop, yelling and waving his arms wildly.

The horses' heads jerked up and they bolted, shying away from him and starting at a dead run, their heads pointed to the west. At the same moment, the other three braves emerged from concealment, all of them pounding toward the eastern edges of the herd and pushing them in the opposite direction.

An explosion of dust erupted in front of his pony's hoofs. The animal shied, and Kaytennae nearly fell off its back. He grabbed a handful of the pony's mane and righted himself, at the same time searching for the source of the bullet that had nearly unhorsed him.

There. One of the vaqueros rode at breakneck speed in from a draw on the south side of the pasture. He had his carbine at his shoulder, pointed at Kaytennae.

Hooking his left knee over his pony's flank, Kaytennae ducked behind the neck of his horse and aimed his gun at the vaquero. He fired, and the vaquero tumbled from his mount and rolled over and over in the grass until at last he lay still.

By then the horses were moving as a herd, dashing headlong across the pasture to the west, just as the Apaches intended. The four kept pushing the herd across the plain, aiming for the low foothills of the Candelaria range. Once among the ravines and switchbacks, they would be both harder to find and harder to follow.

After the sun had moved maybe two hand-widths across the sky, they came to a small ciénega at the neck of a canyon. They slowed and allowed the horses to drink.

"I killed one of the vaqueros," said the boy who had held the horses. "I wanted to take his scalp, but the horses were running away."

"It is good you did not try," Kaytennae said. "There was no time for that. Another time, maybe soon, you will have plenty of chances to count coup on your enemies—if they do not kill you first. Today we have to get these horses to the people. That is the most important thing." He did not say anything about the vaquero he had killed; it was not important.

He looked up at the sun. "They have had enough water," he told his men. "We have to keep moving."

Chapter 9

By the time they got back to the Ysleta headquarters, Wiswall and Andrews felt as if not only their gear and clothes were coated with dust, but their windpipes as well. August was more than half finished, but the heat coming off the rocks and alkaline flats made them think winter was never coming again.

They had been back about a week when a distinguished looking Mexican, accompanied by three heavily armed vaqueros, rode into the yard of the Ranger headquarters. Sitting in a small patch of shade from the roof overhang of the Rangers' assembly building, Andrews watched as the man dismounted from his smartly caparisoned palomino, handed the reins to one of his attendants, and walked with measured pace toward Lieutenant Baylor's front steps.

After he had been inside for a few minutes, the front door opened and Lieutenant Baylor poked his head out the door. He looked around for a few seconds, and finally spotted Andrews, lounging with his back against the wall. "Joseph, would you be kind enough to ask Sergeant Gillett to step over here, please?"

Andrews pulled himself upright and walked inside. This West Texas heat made him feel limp all the time.

He hadn't noticed it so much when they had been riding on patrol, hunting Victorio. Maybe the Mexican had brought with him a summons to some sort of action. A little to his own surprise, Andrews realized he hoped that was the case. At the moment, anything seemed preferable to withering slowly in the unremitting glare of the never-ending summer.

Sergeant Gillett sat at one of the plank tables in the common room, cleaning a Colt revolver. He looked up as Andrews approached.

"Lieutenant Baylor is asking for you, Sergeant. And there's a Mexican fellow in there with him."

Gillett looked a question at him.

"Older fellow, kind of tall. Just got here, and three other men with him. Looks like somebody important."

Gillett nodded. He carefully wrapped an oiled rag around the disassembled action of his revolver and set it on a shelf on the wall behind him. "Thank you, James. I'll head on over right now."

Andrews felt Shep nosing his hand and kneeled down to pet the dog.

"What's doing?" Wiswall said from where he sat, slouched in the corner with his hat pulled down over his eyes.

"Not sure," Andrews said. "Mexican fellow just rode in with three vaqueros, all of them packing a fair amount of iron. He walked into Baylor's house, and then Baylor asked for the sergeant."

Wiswall poked the front of his hat up and gave Andrews a studying look. "News about Victorio?"

"Could be. When last we heard, he was still on the other side of the river, someplace. Maybe they bagged him, and they've come to tell the lieutenant the glad tidings."

"Or maybe they haven't, and they've come to ask for our help again."

"Your guess is as good as mine. I calculate we'll hear something whenever Baylor decides to tell us."

The answer came a half-hour later, as Sergeant Gillett walked into the common room and said, "Men, look to your gear. We're riding south as soon as preparations can be completed. You'll want to pack for a long patrol."

"Well, there you go," Wiswall said. "I can't think of anything that would be taking us south in such a hurry, unless it's Victorio."

Andrews shrugged. "Makes sense. Now, if I can just remember where I left my parasol."

The Mexican's name was Don Ramón Arranda, and as Andrews and Wiswall soon learned, he was the *comandante* of the volunteer patrols in northern Chihuahua. Victorio had attacked the rancho of Don Mariano Samaniego-Delgado, he told them, and Don Mariano, with the agreement of the provincial governor, had formally requested the assistance of the Texas Rangers and the army of the *norteamericanos* to bring the renegade chief to justice.

"Victorio stole many *caballos* from Don Mariano," Don Ramón said, "and he killed two of Don Mariano's vaqueros. We believe he is hiding in the Candelarias, and, with all the animals he has just taken, maybe he is planning a new raid."

By now, Andrews and Wiswall had become not only accustomed to, but directly involved in the Ranger troop's preparation for a patrol. This was not the quick departure of times past, however, because the campaign against Victorio was being coordinated among the United States Army, the Texas Rangers, and the Mexican provincial militia. By the time Lieutenant Baylor had his final orders, the calendar had inched past the end of August into early September.

Not that this made much difference in the heat. As Wiswall tugged tight the final buntline hitch on a mule's packsaddle, he pulled an already-soaked red bandanna out of his hip pocket and mopped the sweat out of his eyes. "Lord a' mighty, how did we ever survive July, if it's still this hot in September?" he said.

One of other Rangers, walking past with a saddle on his shoulder, gave a low chuckle. "Sweat's good for you, Wiz. Keeps the poisons out of your blood."

"Well, at least my corpse will be detoxified when I fall out of the saddle with sunstroke."

"Might want to top off your canteen. I doubt it'll cool off as we ride into Mexico." The other man continued on his way.

Wiswall grimaced inwardly. Part of him—a very small part—wondered if he and Andrews had made the right decision, staying here to ride with the Rangers against Victorio. There were other places they could be going, other faces they could be seeing.

For the third time that day, he wondered why he still had no return letter from Annie. He wondered if she was still in Leadville, singing at the opera house that she had mentioned as her next destination during the only brief conversation the two of them had actually had. He wondered how many forlorn letters from lonely men she had gotten before she received his—if any of them had even reached her at all. If she had left Leadville, where had she gone? He had to find a way to talk to her—at least once. But how could he? And what made him think she would listen or care what he had to say?

With Aniceto Duran in the lead, accompanied by his uncle, Bernardo Olguin—brother of the slain Simon Olguin—the Rangers rode out of the Ysleta station and down the river road toward the village of Socorro. The eastern sky, ahead of them, had not yet begun graying toward dawn, but the air still held the warmth of the day before; it would soon heat up for the day ahead.

For a good while, the only sounds were the squeaking of saddle leather, the muted jingling of bits, and the clopping of shod hooves on summer-baked clay. They rode two abreast, with Baylor at the front of the Rangers and Gillett bringing up the rear of the column of thirteen riders.

Shep, as was his habit, paced the two Indian scouts at the very front. Glancing every which way and often looking back to assure himself the Ranger column still followed, the black shepherd occasionally stopped a moment to sniff before trotting on.

Down the southern Ysleta grade, past the frequent trails, rivulets, bypasses, byroads, and byways, the troopers rode along the Rio Grande plain. As Wiswall rocked along in his saddle, he pondered the mission that lay ahead of them. If it went as intended, Victorio and most or all of his people would be dead at the end of it. The thought ground in his gut. Without doubt, Victorio was a desperate man who had shown himself, time and again, capable of vicious reprisal against any who opposed him. He had stolen horses and cattle, killed ranchers, travelers, and soldiers who crossed his path, and either ordered or at least permitted the torture of those enemies unfortunate enough to be taken alive by his fighters.

And yet, on the cold and desolate plain of Crow Flat, Wiswall had stood face to face with the Apache chief and watched as he decided to allow a whole troop of surrounded, hopelessly outnumbered Texas Rangers to ride away unharmed. He had done this, as far as Wiswall could tell, for no reason other than that the Rangers, at Wiswall's and Andrews' bidding, had put themselves at risk in order to rescue the stranded Shep. Something about this act of compassion and courage had touched a chord in the renegade chief's heart. Wiswall, Andrews, Shep, and the rest of the Rangers were still alive as a result.

So now they rode to kill him. The two opposing notions jangled together in Wiswall's mind; he could not reconcile them. As he had listened at Crow Flat, Victorio had recited a few of his grievances against the whites and their government. By any measure, it was not an inconsiderable list. For about the thousandth time, Wiswall asked himself: if he were in Victorio's place, would he not do much the same as the chief had done? Would he sit on a barren, disease-infested reservation, far from the mountainsides and clear, flowing streams of his home country, and watch his people die, the ears and eyes of the whites shut against their suffering? Or would he try to do something about it?

Wiswall wondered what would happen if he once again found himself in Victorio's presence. In his mind, he could still see the chief's rugged, weathered face: the flat, hooded gaze, like that of a stalking cougar; the long, unbraided hair falling down either side of his broad cheekbones; the wide mouth, set in a line as straight as the desert horizon. Would Victorio's face be the last thing Wiswall ever saw? Or would it be the other way around?

The coming day drew a dim blue line along the eastern skyline. They had ridden through Socorro in the dark and now were coming into the outskirts of San Elizario. A Mexican driving an oxcart pulled over to the side as the Rangers rode past; a few people were stirring by now. In the darkness ahead, Wiswall saw the flickering of a cook fire; he smelled the sweetish scent of the wood smoke drifting up on the easy south breeze. They would reach the ferry crossing at El Porvenir by noon, if all went according to plan. Then they would cross into Mexico, where, somewhere in the rough country between El Paso del Norte and Ciudad Chihuahua, Victorio waited.

Wiswall felt his fingers straying toward the Colt revolver holstered at his side. He pulled his hand away and tried to think about something else.

Chapter 10

"We'll dismount for a short rest and let the horses and mules drink at the town well," Baylor said. "Then we'll be on our way."

San Elizario was a village of adobe houses of varied sizes. Wiswall always thought the place looked like it had sprouted on its own from the drab, brown clay of the land that surrounded it. About a hundred people lived here, most of them *peones* or, at the very most, smallholders with a cow, a donkey or two, and a few acres of beans or alfalfa irrigated from the river.

The center of the village was a small, green space shaded by craggy cottonwoods and screened here and there by the lacy leaves of the rugged mesquite. One of the men went to the stone-rimmed well and started drawing water for the animals, pouring it by the hide bucketful into the clay troughs that surrounded the well.

As the men dismounted and stretched their legs and lower backs, one of the town elders approached. Following him were two young women carrying baskets.

"Señor *teniente*, thank you for ridding this land of *los Indios malos*. You and your Rangers have our gratitude."

After this little speech, the two young women came forward and offered each of the men some of the contents of the baskets: freshly picked figs.

"You have a long way to ride," the old man said. "Maybe these *higos* will taste even sweeter when the sun is hot and the trail is dusty."

"Friend, I thank you sincerely, on behalf of all my men," Lieutenant Baylor said, making a little bow. "We will do our best to help make San Elizario a safe place for you and your people."

"Gracias, señor," the old man said, bobbing his head. "Muchas gracias."

"I guess the word is out," Andrews said, coming up beside Wiswall.

"For all we know, Victorio heard about it when we rode out this morning," Wiswall said. "All the same, a fresh fig or two will be a nice way to help the beef jerky slide down a little easier."

"Couldn't hurt."

With the animals watered and canteens topped off, the Rangers were back in the saddle and moving down the road by the time the sun's disk had cleared the eastern horizon. Wiswall and Andrews found themselves riding along just in front of Sergeant Gillett.

"The folks in San Elizario seem eager to see the last of Victorio, from what I can tell," Andrews said.

"Oh, certainly," Gillett said, nodding. "The Mexicans on both sides of the Rio Grande have taken more than their share of abuse from Victorio and his raiders. I think you fellows probably heard a little about what happened to the men from Carrizal, last November, didn't you?"

"That was just before we got here," Wiswall said. "But I knew that some men rode out to try to recover some stolen horses and walked straight into an ambush, and then, a few days later, when a rescue party came along, they met the same fate as the first bunch."

Gillett nodded grimly. "We rode to Carrizal at the head of nearly a hundred men—from Saragosa, Tres Jacales, San Ygnacio, all over—bent on finding and punishing Victorio for this crime. They asked Lieutenant Baylor to come, and we readily agreed, knowing if we didn't fight him south of the river, it was only a matter of time before we'd be fighting him north of it.

"Of course Victorio, from his perch at the top of the Candelarias, could see us coming from nearly the time we left El Paso, just as he had seen the men coming from Carrizal. In the face of our numbers, he just faded away into the mountains, and we never found him. But we surely found where he had been.

"Victorio laid his trap in a narrow defile leading up into the mountains: a place with plenty of cover on both sides. When the men from Carrizal rode far enough into the canyon that there was no easy retreat, the Apaches opened fire. It was a slaughter.

"I found where one Mexican had crawled in among the rocks and was able to shield himself from any fire coming from east or west. But his legs were exposed to the Apaches on the north face of the canyon, and they had shot his legs off, up to the knees. I saw a place where seven men of Carrizal were killed, and in the rocks above, I found the sign of a single Apache who had apparently shot them all; there was a single, neat little pile of twenty-seven cartridges. He had perched there and picked them off, one by one."

"I guess they gave up on their stolen horses after that," Andrews said.

Gillett shook his head. "Twenty-nine husbands,

brothers, and fathers of Carrizal would never come back. Our return to the little village was one of the most mournful occasions I expect I'll ever live through."

Wiswall kept quiet and stared straight ahead. Out of the corner of his eye, Andrews studied his partner for a few seconds. "Sergeant, what do you know about the weather in the south of California?" he said.

"Well, I can't say as I know too much about it, one way or the other. I've heard that a lot of folks came through here back around '49 and '50, headed out that direction to make a quick fortune. But I was too young to be among them, of course. Why do you ask?"

"Well, Wiswall and I were thinking that we might ride out there and see about prospects. I've heard the weather is considerably milder, in some parts at least, than hereabout. I could do with a little relief from heat for awhile, truth be told."

Gillett chuckled. "And last January, you were complaining about the cold."

"With good reason," Wiswall chimed in. "It was a long, cold walk back to Ysleta from Crow Flat. I had about decided I'd never be warm again."

Gillett laughed aloud. "You boys looked pretty pitiful by the time you got back here."

"Five railroads are practically at the doorstep of El Paso," Wiswall said, "and the Southern Pacific is already operating all up and down, between San Francisco and the southern part of the state. The way Andrews and I see it, a man could make a comfortable sum for himself, if he gets out there before all the land has been bought up."

"I don't doubt it," Gillett said. "But I reckon I've already got deep roots in Texas."

"How long before you pop the question to Helen Baylor, Sergeant?" Andrews said.

The sergeant gave Andrews a sharp look.

"Now, Sergeant, please don't take offense," Andrews said, smiling. "But a blind man could tell that you're sweet on her, and, if I'm not badly misled, the feeling seems to be returned."

Gillett allowed a guilty smile to creep onto his face, and it looked like he was trying to tuck his chin into the blue bandanna around his neck. "Well, I guess you've got me dead to rights, Jim," he said. "I do confess to having a strong admiration for Miss Helen's feminine traits."

"Nothing in the world wrong with that," Andrews said. "My partner here has had his head turned by a spirited young opera singer by the name of Annie. Isn't that right, Wiswall?"

Wiswall gave Andrews a sour look. "Andrews only hoo-raws me over it because no woman in her right mind would give him a second look."

Andrews laughed. "Now, Wiswall, don't take me wrong. Have I ever said the first word against Annie? Hell, I've carried more than one letter to the post for you. And remind me—how many letters have you gotten in return?"

Wiswall muttered the nastiest epithet he could think of and stared pointedly away from his partner.

"William, I think our friend, Mr. Andrews, here, might be an incorrigible bachelor. What do you think?" Gillett said, grinning.

"I think there's a shorter term for it," Wiswall said, still frowning.

Gillett and Andrews both laughed.

"Seriously though, fellows," Gillett said a bit later, "will you really leave us for the wilds of southern California? I thought maybe we had made Texas Rangers of you, more or less permanently."

"Sergeant, riding with you and Lieutenant Baylor has been a privilege and an honor," Wiswall said. "I think even Andrews agrees with me; this has been an unforgettable experience that we will look back upon continually, for the rest of our days."

Andrews nodded.

"But don't you sometimes wonder, Sergeant?" Wiswall said.

Gillett's face tilted a question toward Wiswall.

"What's out there? How far can you go? What might you find when you got there?"

Gillett rode a while, his brow knitted in thought. "I guess I don't think about that, so much, nowadays. There was a time, maybe. But now, it always seems like there's the next thing to be done."

Wiswall nodded. "I understand. And I believe that the next thing for us is out west. As far west as we can get. Maybe we'll stop there, maybe we won't. But we've got to go out there to find out."

After a while, Gillett said, "Well, fellows, whatever you find on the other side of that next hillside, I hope it's to your liking."

Andrews shrugged. "Probably too much to hope for, but thank you, Sergeant."

As the sun neared its zenith, they were approaching the low-water crossing of the Rio Grande at the Mexican village of El Porvenir. Across the river from it, the army was in the process of establishing a rude camp, in support of the cavalry operations in pursuit of Victorio. As the Rangers rode near, they could see the pole-and-wattle ramadas that had been thrown up to shield the canvas tents of the Buffalo Soldiers from the unremitting glare of the West Texas sun and to provide a little extra protection during the rare downpours. There was a rude corral of stacked stone and cottonwood poles that looked to be holding about thirty assorted horses and mules, all bearing the "US" brand on their hindquarters.

"Men, let's dismount and give the animals another good drink before we cross the river," Lieutenant Baylor said when the detail had gathered at the edge of the army encampment. "We'll eat here, and I'll reconnoiter with the officer in command."

They learned that the soldiers occupying the camp were from Company K of the Tenth Cavalry, with a few elements of the Signal Corps mixed in. It was a pretty small posting, commanded by a Lieutenant Woodward. The soldiers were an agreeable lot; they welcomed the Rangers to sit in the shade of their ramadas while they ate their cold biscuits and jerky.

Woodward told Lieutenant Baylor that there had been no sign of Victorio's people thereabout since the previous month, when he had crossed the river after raiding Jesus Cota's rancho and killing his herdsman. "We've had our scouts out in every direction for twenty or twenty-five miles," he told Baylor, "and not seen hide nor hair. Not that I'm grieved over that, you understand."

Baylor nodded. "We're headed across the river today, joining up with the *milicianos* and, if I'm not mistaken, a detachment of the Ninth Cavalry, to try and rid the country of Victorio, once and for all."

"Well, Lieutenant, I wish you godspeed in that errand," Lieutenant Woodward said. "I'll be heartily glad to return to patrolling the railroad routes and dealing with the odd stagecoach robbery."

Baylor chuckled. "Well, Old Vic has led us a merry chase for coming on a year now," he said. "He's a wily one, and no two ways about it. But surely we can hem him up, this time."

The Rangers led their mounts down to the river and allowed them to drink their fill from the water running across the gravel bar of the crossing, slow and warm in the bright sunlight. They devoured their noon rations and a few of them leaned up against the rickety corner posts of the ramadas and dozed for a few precious minutes before Lieutenant Baylor gave the command to mount up. With Aniceto and his uncle leading the way, the Texas Rangers splashed across the Rio Grande and climbed slowly up the easy grade on the Mexican side.

Chapter 11

"**M**ake sure you tell the women and children—all of them that are old enough to walk—to keep their kits with them, all the time," Victorio said to the men seated in front of him. "We have a long way to go and many enemies between us and safety. Even when they lie down to sleep, all the people must have their food with them, and their weapons. Even the smallest girl must carry a knife and keep it sharp. They must keep their kits tied to their belts and always have their blankets and robes with them. They must not lay any of it aside, ever. We do not know when the enemy may come upon us, even in the night."

He looked at them. Did any of them—other than Nana—understand what he was saying? Did any of them understand that this could very well be their last march as free people?

They had waited as long as they could for any word of compromise from the whites. Until the last moment—and maybe beyond—Victorio had hoped that someone among them would listen to reason and allow the Chihenne to return to their ancestral lands around Ojo Caliente. Before, when men like Michael Steck and Charles Drew had been in charge of the reservations,

Victorio had been able to reason with them. The men who came after them, though, had ears of stone.

And so, no word had come, and the enemy was encircling him. Terrazos was bringing many *milicianos*; the bluecoats were preparing to cross the Rio Grande; the Texas Rangers had already forded at El Porvenir and were riding toward him.

They had to go to Juh and his Chiricahua people in the Blue Mountains, far to the west. Only there, among the crags and passes of the high country could they expect to find a place of refuge. Victorio had done everything he could think of, but none of it was enough.

"We will divide into three bands, and each group will take a different trail. I will lead the main warrior group; Kaytennae, you will pick thirty men to stay with the women and children; and Nana, you will come behind with a few fighters. Each night, we will decide where the day's march will end, and each leader will decide his own route to get there. We will all leave trail signs for each other.

"There is good water and grass to the south, at the place the Mexicans call Tres Castillos. We will make for there first, to give our animals a chance to drink and eat before we make the crossing to the Blue Mountains. Maybe our sign will also disguise from our foes the place we mean to go, at least for a few more days.

"Tell the women to begin cutting and drying as much meat as they can. We will take some cattle when we get there; we will eat as much as we can and dry the rest for the final journey to Juh."

His eyes roved the seated figures before him. "This is my plan. Now, I want to know what you think. Kaytennae, is there wisdom in my words?"

The younger man looked carefully at Victorio for

several seconds. He nodded. "I will do everything you have said, Bidu-ya. My men and I will keep the women and children safe as we travel. If the Mexicans or the bluecoats come, we will hide them until it is safe to move again."

Victorio nodded. "Nana, you have led warriors and scouts through this country for many seasons. Will you follow this plan? Does it seem good to you?"

The older man looked at the ground for a long time. Finally, he looked up at Victorio. "Bidu-ya, the troubles of these past few years are greater than any we have ever faced. And always, you have kept the people fed and given them water to drink. You have stayed ahead of the whites and the brown coats, and when we had to fight, you have helped us fight well and lose no more men than necessary. You are a good chief. I will follow you to Tres Castillos and on to Juh's stronghold in the Blue Mountains."

Victorio nodded slowly. "Then it is decided. Go back and tell your families and your young men. We will stay here one more day, and while it is still dark tomorrow night, we will begin moving south."

When the men had gone, Victorio went to find his granddaughter. Liluye was helping one of the women peel meat into thin strips that could be hung on the bushes for drying. She looked up at his approach and smiled.

"You are working. That is good," he said. "We will need food that we can eat on the trail."

"We are going to join Juh, they say," Liluye said, turning back to her work. "Is it a long way, Grandfather?"

"It is far enough. But with food to eat and good horses, we can get there."

"Will we be safe when we are there, Grandfather?"

He watched her nimble fingers tugging the strips of meat loose as she wielded the knife. He watched the red, glistening meat as she laid it across the branches of cenizo and scrub oak. She worked without pausing, without looking up at him, even though he paused long in his answer. He thought about Liluye's mother, dead from the sickness that had ravaged his people on the cursed reservation at San Carlos.

"It will be better to be with Juh. So finish your work, Liluye, and then we can ride without empty bellies."

From San Ygnacio they rode in, dusty and trail-weary, armed with everything from old dragoon revolvers to battered double-barreled shotguns. From the villages along the Rio Grande, from Tres Jacales, Socorro, and Guadalupe del Rio, they came in answer to the summons from Don Ramón, to whom many of them owed debts of obligation, if not outright servitude. They came to his ranch at San Marcos de Cantarica, at the northern edge of the Llano de los Castillos, ready to go out with the Texas Rangers and fight the dreaded Victorio—for the last time, they hoped.

Andrews and Wiswall watched them gathering: some of them old enough to be grandfathers, and others who had yet to trim their beards for the first time.

"General Terrazas is said to be coming up from Chihuahua City with a force of some three hundred men, including cavalry and infantry," Lieutenant Baylor had told them at that morning's assembly. "In addition, Colonel Buell, from Fort Cummings, is proceeding south with men from the Fifteenth Infantry. With the hundred men we have arriving here, we will ride south, gradually intersecting with Colonel Buell's line of march. Our aim is to catch Victorio in a three-pronged pincer."

But first they had to find him. All indications were that after their unsuccessful attempt to take control of Rattlesnake Springs, the Apaches had crossed the river and gone into hiding in the Candelaria range, which had successfully shielded them in the past. But now, the Apache and Navajo scouts were reporting that the band had taken to moving about in some pattern that did not precisely fit with any of its previous habits.

Meanwhile, Shep had ensconced himself at Don Ramón's hacienda much in the manner of a grand personage. Since the Rangers' arrival two days earlier, he had staked out a spot just outside the back door of the *cocina*. There, in the shade afforded by an arbor of trailing white clematis, he had little more to do than catch in his jaws and gulp down the choice morsels tossed to him by the smiling kitchen girls. There was hardly a time of day when one of the bright-eyed children of the hacienda was not playing with him, fawning over him, or drawing a fresh bowl of water from the cistern to bring to him.

"If we don't ride out of here in a day or two, we'll have lost Shep for good, I warrant," Andrews remarked to Wiswall as they squatted against the adobe wall of the courtyard, eating the still-warm tamales Don Ramón's servants had served up for the midday meal. "For one thing, he'll be too fat for the trail."

Wiswall chuckled. "Well, it's hard to begrudge the old boy a little easy duty, for once."

Andrews nodded. "True enough. That will come to an end soon enough, won't it?"

The Rangers, augmented by the more than one hundred Mexican volunteers raised by Don Ramón, rode away from the hacienda the next day, as the sun began to settle onto the western horizon. They were instructed to scout the flanks of the Itancheria range to discover, if possible, some trace of Victorio's movements. The keen-eyed Aniceto and his uncle found evidence of the passage of a group of unshod ponies, but because of the gathering darkness and the effects of a recent local downpour, they were unable to decipher how many Apaches had been in the party.

As the men made camp for the night, Sergeant Gillett approached Lieutenant Baylor. "There are three fires that look to be in the hills east of the Arranda hacienda," he said. "At first light, let me scout over that way with a few men to see if some of Victorio's people are over there."

Baylor nodded. "Take five Rangers and ten Mexican volunteers with you. Maybe we can catch up to the old scoundrel sooner, rather than later. But if you encounter a force of any size, do not engage; send a rider back to me and we will bring the main patrol along as quickly as possible."

At first light, Gillett, accompanied by Andrews, Wiswall, Shep, two other Rangers, and ten of Don Ramón's men, rode quietly away from the camp, headed northeast. As they crossed the dry country, they scoured the terrain in front of them for any sign of the passage of Victorio's band. By midday, they were nearing the slopes of the Sierra de Los Piños when they heard hoofbeats behind them and coming fast.

It was a rider from Lieutenant Baylor, sent to tell them to immediately break off their reconnaissance of the signal fires and go with all speed to the Rancheria Hills, just north of Chihuahua City. "Some of the Navajos cut sign leading that direction. They think Vic might be headed there, and they want you to reach the hills ahead of him and prevent his passage, if possible." Gillett looked around at the men. "All right, you heard the order," he said. "If we ride south at a brisk trot, we can make Cerro Rancheria before sundown. Get a quick drink, and we'll eat in the saddle."

Wiswall groaned inwardly. How he wished he were back at Don Ramón's hacienda, eating warm tamales and watching Shep lounge beneath the clematis vine.

Chapter 12

Peering ahead through the dusty haze, Andrews and Wiswall could see the tiny, adobe building that marked the Lucero stage stand, on the Chihuahua City–El Paso del Norte road. The outlines of the box-shaped hut wavered in the heat rising from the Llano de los Castillos. Its walls were the same color as the baked terrain, and at times in the heat-shimmer, they seemed to disappear, as if they had melted back into the landscape from which they were raised.

"Lord a' mighty, I hope there's a cistern at that stage stand, at least," Andrews said, pulling his hat brim lower against the merciless glare. "Do you reckon they've forgotten how to have winter in Mexico?"

"Easy there, partner," Wiswall said. "Why are you in such a rush? It's only the end of September, after all. Best to enjoy this balmy, shirtsleeve weather while we've got it."

Gillett and his party arrived at the stage stand about a half-hour after the main body of Baylor's command, from the look of it. As soon as the sergeant swung down from his horse, Lieutenant Baylor stepped from the doorway of the adobe hut.

"I see my rider reached you."

Gillett took a long pull from his canteen and nodded his head. "Yes, sir. We had just taken up our positions in the hills above Ojo Laguna. We were waiting for Vic to show up, but your messenger got there first. So, at first light, we came on here as quickly as we could." Baylor looked around at the rest of the patrol. "Thank you, men. *Muchas gracias.* But now we have reliable information that Victorio is back up in the country outside Carrizal, where he was hiding at first."

"For a man with that many mouths to feed, he sure is mobile," Andrews said.

Baylor nodded. "He is a past master at concealing his movements and his location. Not only we, but the Mexican militia and our own army have been scouring the country on both sides of the river for much of the past year, looking for him. We have to follow every lead, I'm afraid. And this is the best one we have, right now."

Baylor turned back toward Gillett. "Sergeant, tell your men to water their horses and themselves. Let's give ourselves a little more rest." He squinted up at the sun. "Looks like we've got about three hours of daylight left. We'll start our ride north to Carrizal after sundown. Maybe it will be a little cooler."

"That would be welcome," Wiswall said.

"I don't see how it could get any hotter," Andrews said.

Since the company numbered nearly a hundred armed and mounted men, Baylor judged they had little to fear from a sneak attack, especially at night when the Apaches were typically loath to fight. So, their night march took them up the road that connected Chihuahua City and El Paso del Norte. There was no worry about footing for the horses, and no risk of getting off course.

But it was still a bone-wearying ride. In order to cover the more than ninety miles that lay between the Lucero stage stand and the village of Carrizal, the Rangers and their Mexican allies had to ride at a brisk trot, almost non-stop, from sundown until the next morning. By the time they arrived in Carrizal, the sun had cleared the horizon.

As they sagged onto the stone wall surrounding the well in the center of town where the men were watering their horses, Wiswall and Andrews saw one of the Mexican volunteers speaking with an old man of the village. The *abuelo* was shaking his head and pointing east. "*Los indios han ido hacia el amanecer,*" he said. "*No estan aquí ahora.*"

"I'm pretty sure I understood that last part," Andrews said. "Sounds like we got here too late."

Wiswall groaned.

"Victorio may run us all into the ground, trying to catch him," Andrews said. "Hell, maybe that was his plan the whole time."

When the horses had all been watered and the men had rested for a few minutes, Lieutenant Baylor gathered them beside the well. "Well, our foe has once again shown his cunning—or possibly his desperation. Local scouts have reported the movement of a large group of Apaches toward the east, starting late yesterday. It is not the habit of Apaches to travel at night, especially with women and children, so it seems that we may be able to pick up the trail before we go too far.

"Let's eat some breakfast and rest for an hour or two, and then we will resume the pursuit."

But once again, circumstances conspired against them. Less than ten miles east of Carrizal, a sudden thunderstorm burgeoned upward on the desert thermals. It rolled in over the hills to the west of the patrol and swept down upon them from behind. The rain, driven by gusts of wind from the fast-moving storm, drenched the riders and their horses and turned the Chihuahuan desert into a morass of mud and brown rivulets; the trail was lost.

"Well, that ought to have cooled you off some," Wiswall said to Andrews as they rode along, wringing out soaked bandannas and dumping rainwater from hats.

"Likely, the sun will come right back out and steam us like cabbage."

"You just can't find the bright side, can you, partner?"

Baylor called a halt not long after the squall had passed over them. "Well, we can't follow a trail we can't see," he said. "Señor Gutierrez," he said, addressing one of the older men among the volunteers, "you are more familiar with this country than I; what would you advise, now?"

Gutierrez peered away toward the east and thought for several seconds. "Señor Teniente, I think that Victorio tries to take his people to the Sierra de los Piños, maybe. Or maybe he tries to go to Laguna Grande, on the other side. He knows that in the mountains, he is harder to find, and like all of us, he must have water for his animals and his people."

Baylor looked at Gillett. "Sergeant, do you have any ideas?"

Gillett shook his head. "We've been following him, from pillar to post and back again, for three days now, and haven't seen hide nor hair. He's already headed east; seems like keeping on in that direction makes the most sense."

They trailed along toward the east for the rest of the morning and into the early afternoon, and to their relief, they were able to pick up the trail of the Apaches again once they reached a stretch of country that had avoided most of the heavy rainfall as the storm had tracked south of their line of travel. Carefully observing the dim traces of their quarry's passing, they rode on into the late afternoon.

As they climbed a rocky rise, Shep, from his vantage point in front of the column of riders, twitched his head suddenly erect and sifted the air with his nose. He scampered to the top of the rise and stood there, sending a shower of barks down the slope.

At the sound of Shep's barking, Andrews and Wiswall loosened their rifles in their saddle scabbards. "Last time he did that, we had a social call from Victorio," Wiswall said.

"I hadn't forgotten." Andrews spurred his horse ahead to the front of the column, where Baylor waited, having halted his mount to stare upward at Shep.

"What do you believe he's trying to tell us, James?" the lieutenant said, pointing with his chin toward the dog.

"I'm not certain, Lieutenant, but I sure do believe I'd approach the top of this hill with all due caution."

Baylor nodded. He turned toward his second-in-command. "Sergeant Gillett, why don't you and Mr. Andrews slip up there on foot and see what's to be seen? Meanwhile, we'll keep a careful eye out back here to make sure our canine friend isn't distracted while someone else slips up on us from behind."

Gillett and Andrews dismounted and handed the reins of their horses to some of the other men. Splitting up and stooping low, the two men made their way to the top of the slope while endeavoring to keep themselves concealed from whatever waited on the other side. By this time, Shep's barking had subsided, but his attention was still focused on whatever had initially captured it. Andrews poked his head around the base of a large rock conveniently settled at the crest of the rise. Below him were about a dozen horses, some of them looking uphill at Shep, and others nosing about for such forage as presented itself. Andrews and Gillett peered about for several minutes, but no riders for the horses—Apache or otherwise—could be seen.

They reported back to Baylor, and the column rode to the top of the rise. "Those horses are shod, if my ears don't betray me," the lieutenant said, studying the scene.

"Sí, Teniente, these are no *caballos de los indios*," Miguel Guttierez said, riding up beside Baylor. "These animals belong to Don Mariano, I think. Maybe they were part of the herd Victorio stole, but they have gotten loose."

"Well, we'll bring them along with us," Baylor said. "I imagine we'll be able to put them to good use, at some point." Some of the volunteers dropped loops over the necks of the stray horses, and they came along with the column without much fuss.

Afraid of losing the scant trail in the dark, Baylor called a halt as the sunset purpled into night. "We'll camp here and pick up the chase again in the morning," he announced.

They set sentries, and Baylor gave the nod to a couple of small cooking fires. "Our numbers are sufficient that Victorio will think twice about attacking, even if he did decide to fight at night. It's been a long, difficult chase so far, and not too successful, at that. Some warm grub will do us all good."

The men indeed seemed heartened by this decision. One of the Rangers actually made biscuits, and some of the Mexicans patted tortillas out of corn meal and water and baked them on heated stones before rolling them around boiled beans. They washed it all down with coffee.

After the meal was consumed, the cooking utensils wiped and stowed, and here and there a cigarette rolled and lit, one of the Mexican volunteers began to sing. The man had a pleasant, high voice, and the longer he sang, the quieter the others became.

He came to the end of the song, and after a reflective pause, Wiswall said, "That was beautiful, amigo. But my Spanish is *muy malo*, and I couldn't make out the meaning—though I'm pretty sure I heard the word 'Victorio' in there, a time or two."

The singer smiled and stared into the dying fire. "Yes, it is a song of our enemy, the man we are chasing and trying to kill. If I put the words in English . . . " He thought for a moment more, then slowly recited,

I am the Indian Victorio.
It is my passion to fight.
I must attain glory,
And I will make the world tremble.

I want to live; I want to die.
To live, so I can fight.
To Mexico I'll go;
I'll go to fight
And shout "War! War!"
Until I die.
I am the Indian Victorio.

Wiswall sat unmoving. The other men were silent. Even Shep was still, his eyes fixed on the singer, who continued to stare into the fire.

The words ran around and around in Wiswall's mind, even as the other men prepared their bedrolls or curled up on the ground beneath their *serapes.* The fire died down to coals, and still he sat, with the song of Victorio swirling around and around inside him.

I want to live . . . I want to die . . . "War! War!" until I die . . . I am the Indian Victorio . . .

When he opened his eyes the next morning, the song was still in his mind, pinned there like the smell of fresh water. The song, and Victorio's face as he had seen it on the cold, windy plain at Crow Flat.

Chapter 13

Victorio watched as the women and older children gathered the dead branches lying beneath the honey mesquites along the edges of the draw. He turned to Nana.

"Make sure they cover the trail as you keep on toward Tres Castillos. I will take my men and ride back toward Candelaria. We will try to draw the Rangers and Mexicans after us. We will lose them in the broken country and double back to come to Tres Castillos. Let the people rest as much as you can, but keep moving steadily and in small groups."

Nana nodded. "We will find the cached supplies at Tres Castillos, and we will wait for you."

Victorio signaled to the mounted warriors, and they rode away in a cloud of dust, to the mouth of the ravine and then angling away toward the northwest. As he rode, he looked back a final time at Nana, his few old men, and the women and children. Victorio hoped he was doing the right thing, taking Kaytennae and his men along with the other fighters. Nana would not be able to put up much of a fight if this trick did not work.

But the enemy drew ever closer. Victorio had to try something different to throw them off the scent. Surely the white-eyes would be more interested in the trail of his fighting men than that of the women and children. He rode forward, his eyes scanning the terrain. The women knew what to do. They would drag the honey mesquite branches behind them, to hide the trail. The Rangers and Mexicans would see the marks of the ponies' hooves and would come after them. There were none of the traitor Apaches or the wily Tiguas with the group that followed him, so Victorio and his people had the advantage of their trailcraft.

It would work. It had to work.

Miguel Guttierez rose from his study of the ground and looked at Lieutenant Baylor. He shrugged. "Señor Teniente, I do not know why *los indios* have turned; all I know is that this is what they have done. They now ride back toward the Candelarias."

Baylor tapped his shooting stick against his leg. He gazed away toward the west and pursed his lips. "I cannot account for it either, Miguel. But I know with certainty that Victorio would not put his warriors afoot. I think we have no choice but to follow where this leads and to keep our eyes and ears open for an ambush."

Gutierrez nodded. "Sí, Teniente, I think it is as you say. Until we have better knowledge, we must follow."

"But we can't keep going indefinitely, Lieutenant," Sergeant Gillett said. "We are running low on water, and the springs and tanks in these parts are undependable—some so alkaline that any man or horse that drinks from them will get plenty sick, if he's lucky. We've got about a day, day-and-a-half of water, and then we're going to start to get in a bad way."

Baylor nodded. "That is true." He stared off to the

west for a few more seconds, then said, "We'll follow him until midday tomorrow. If we haven't caught up with him, we'll turn aside toward Carrizal. We can wait there while we send out riders to see where General Terrazas may be, or if Colonel Buell is drawing near."

Gutierrez nodded. "It is a good plan, Teniente."

"All right, then," Baylor said. "Let's mount up, men, and ride after him. Victorio is a slippery rascal, and no two ways about it, but maybe we'll catch him out, yet."

By noon of the next day, they had reached the Chihuahua City–El Paso del Norte stage road, and there, as plain as day, they saw the prints of a host of unshod ponies. Apparently, Victorio's band had crossed the road, no more than a day earlier; only a single set of northbound stagecoach tracks marred the signs of the Apaches' passing.

"Well, there's nothing else for it, I'm afraid," Baylor said. He gazed in the direction of Victorio's line of travel, shaking his head. "We can't keep going. We'll turn southwest here, and ride to Carrizal. If we keep a steady pace, we ought to get there by dark. Maybe there will be news there, or fresh information."

Still stringing along the recovered Samaniego horses, the column of riders pointed toward Carrizal. They arrived there about an hour after nightfall, covered with dust and nursing raging thirsts, but grateful for a chance to rest, even if for only a day or two.

General Joaquin Terrazas rode into Carrizal on a fine white horse. He was a tall man, standing a quarter-hand taller even than Lieutenant Baylor, and one rarely saw him without a cigarette between his lips.

He rode one horse and had three extras—all white,

also—ever at hand, led by attendants. His uniform was spotless and glittered with brass buttons. He smiled a dazzling smile at the cheering villagers of Carrizal who welcomed his arrival—like a hero who had already vanquished the enemy. Wiswall disliked the general from the moment he saw him.

"Well, he comes from a fine old family, they say," Andrews said as they watched Terrazas's cavalry ride past, all mounted on fine-looking dark horses, well matched in size. "He's been fighting Victorio on this side of the Rio Grande for about as long as we have on our side, and it looks like he brought enough people with him to finish the job, this time."

Along with two hundred mounted cavalry, Terrazas had also brought a hundred infantrymen, most of them Indians of the Tarahumara people, from the mountains of central Mexico.

"They say these Tarahumaras can go for days without water. I've heard some of the Mexicans say that in rough country, they can run a horse into the ground."

"Maybe so," Wiswall grunted. "But the high and mighty general still makes me itch where I can't scratch."

Terrazas's troops were well armed; the cavalry carried carbines and modern sidearms. While less well equipped, the Tarahumaras all had Remington rifled muskets, with bayonets strapped at their sides. All of the men wore multiple belts of ammunition crisscrossing their shoulders. Andrews guessed they each carried as much as two hundred rounds. "They came ready for a scrape, no question," he said.

As they walked among the new arrivals, it became plain to Andrews and Wiswall that they also traveled light. The infantrymen habitually carried only a small bag holding a pound or two of sweetened corn, roughly ground. They could mix this with a little water and make a gruel that could be quickly consumed on the march; such light rations might sustain them for up to a week, even if no other forage was available.

Of course, the *carrizaleños* had no notion that their saviors would need to resort to eating corn mush. On the first night after Terrazas's arrival, there was a huge fiesta in the town square. Two whole beeves and three hogs roasted on spits over deep beds of mesquite coals; the fragrant smoke plumed over the hot, still air of the town, an encircling blanket of enticing aroma. Wiswall calculated that every woman in the village must have been occupied with making tortillas and baking them on one of the dozens of stoneware *comales* he saw employed on the coals of fires built in backyards and in the patios of the larger houses. Everywhere Andrews walked on the day of the celebration, he smelled beans boiling in huge cast-iron pots. The partners calculated that there could not possibly be a chili pepper left anywhere within a ten-mile radius, unless it was currently being chopped, boiled, seared, or otherwise readied to fill the bellies of the people of Carrizal and the military men who had come to rid their region of the dreaded Apache raiders.

On the night of the feast, torches and coal-oil lanterns lit the central square. Some men with battered guitars and fiddles played local tunes—with more enthusiasm than skill—while a few young couples danced. Old women circulated among the smiling throng, serving dipperfuls of homemade *mescal* from crockery pots. The old *señoras* were insistent, too; by the time Andrews figured out how forcefully he needed to decline a refill, his head was already pleasantly abuzz, and the meal wouldn't be served for at least another hour.

Shep was the darling of the entire occasion. He

circulated among the crowd: standing by the musicians one minute, then basking in the attentions of a knot of children, then eagerly sampling the occasional morsel tossed to him by one of the people attending the cooking fires. They shooed the other village dogs away, throwing curses and rocks to send them into retreat with tails curled beneath their bellies. But Shep they welcomed with smiles and fawning and proffered treats. Nothing, it seemed, was too good for *el perro bravo de los Rangers de Tejas.*

"I'm glad to see Shep is watching out for us," Andrews said to Wiswall, nudging his friend and gesturing with his head toward some men carving hunks of steaming meat from the haunch of a beef. "He's tasting the food for us, making sure nobody tries to poison the army."

"His generosity knows no bounds," Wiswall said, smiling and shaking his head. "He's an obsequious old rascal, for sure. Quite incorrigible."

"I wonder if they'll call on him for a speech, after dinner."

Wiswall laughed and allowed one of the passing *señoras* to ladle more *mescal* into his cup.

Thirty paces distant, a man slowly backed away from a knot of villagers and moved beyond the circle of light and gaiety in the Carrizal town plaza. Once hidden by the night, he turned and jogged toward the ravine outside of the village where his pony was tied.

He had to get to Victorio. He had to tell what he had learned.

Chapter 14

"They have Chiricahua with them, and also Navajo," the scout said. "They will not be riding blindly through the hills, following some trail made by an old woman."

Kaytennae spat on the ground. "These Chiricahua who act like hunting dogs for the whites . . . The Navajo I can understand, for they have never loved our people. But the Chiricahua are our blood! If I find one of these serpents in the open country, I will cut open his belly and choke him to death with his own guts!"

The scout looked at Victorio and the other leaders sitting in front of him. "They will find us, Bidu-ya. And they are many. Twenty of their men have more ammunition than all of our fighters, put together."

One of the other men looked at Victorio. "And Terrazas leads them," he said. "His people have been fighting the *nideh* since Nana was a boy. He is no fool."

"The Rangers from Ysleta have come across the river," another said. "They travel with many armed Mexican riders."

Victorio looked at his leaders. "We are not prepared for a pitched battle. The Mescalero Nana sent out to raid for ammunition have not returned. Maybe they have gone back to the reservation. Or maybe they have all been killed."

"We must go to our people," Kaytennae said. "And then we must go to Juh in the Blue Mountains."

Victorio nodded. "Here is my plan. Let us rest here tonight, and in the morning we will start toward Tres Castillos. Then, when the horses have eaten grass and drunk their fill, we will go west, to Juh." He looked around at each of his men, and each of them nodded agreement.

"It is good," Victorio said. "Sleep now, and we will ride before the sun comes up."

The sharp crack of a rifle shot suddenly ricocheted among the ravines. Instinctively, Victorio and his men hunkered down behind whatever cover they could find, searching avidly for the source of the sound. There was no movement.

Then they heard the sound of running horses. Victorio crawled on his belly to peer down towards the ravine where their ponies were hidden: all was still. So, whatever horses were running, they did not belong to his men.

In a few minutes three of the younger men scurried into the camp, peering over their shoulders as they came.

"Bluecoats!" one of them hissed to the others. "We were looking for water near one of the *huecos*, and one of them shot at us."

"We heard the sound of horses running," Victorio said in a low voice.

"The horses and mules of the bluecoats," one of the other young men said. "When he fired his weapon, the noise startled the animals. They started running away, and the bluecoats ran after them. If they had not, we would be trapped beside the *hueco*."

"We cannot ride out in the morning if we do not know where the bluecoats are," Kaytennae said. "We may ride straight into an attack."

"And we do not know how many they are," Victorio said. "We must try to find out where they are camped. Maybe we can get away from here."

In the gray before sunrise, Victorio and Kaytennae watched from concealment as a handful of the bluecoats climbed toward the waterhole where his young men had been spotted the day before. One of them, probably their leader, looked at the dry *hueco*. He studied the surrounding ravine walls and said something quickly to the others. They hurried back downslope, until they were lost to view.

"Never have I seen bluecoats this far south of the river," Victorio breathed. "And this is not all of them; there are many more of them, somewhere—be sure of it." He shook his head. "Our enemies are multiplying; they are all coming to surround us."

"They know we are here," Kaytennae whispered. "We should try to get away."

"We cannot risk having them so close on our trail," Victorio replied. "They do not know where we are concealed. We must keep the ponies quiet. We must wait and watch. Maybe Usen will send us good fortune."

As the sun came up, the bluecoats, their weapons at the ready and their eyes constantly roaming the upper rims of the canyons, pulled back from the mountains. Victorio and his men breathed easier as they watched them riding away.

"I think they are afraid of an ambush," he said to the others. "I think this was a scouting party, and they are going back to their main force."

"Maybe we can slip away now?" Kaytennae said.

"Yes. We must be very careful, but if we do not go now, we will be trapped when they return with the rest of their army. We must go now, while our luck holds."

Baylor and Gillett leaned over the map as General Terrazas pointed. "My men and I have swept through all these regions. Here, in the country around El Carmen . . . and here, here, here—Galeana, Casas Grandes, San Buenaventura—we have scoured the land; my scouts have crawled over the passes and spied out the waterholes. Victorio is not there, and has not been for some time."

"Well, General, if that is the case, then we should sweep the Candelarias," Baylor said. "That looked like where he was headed the last time we had good sign. And now we have enough men that it will be harder for him to slip through a hole in the net."

Terrazas nodded. "This is what I am thinking also, Lieutenant. If we come upon the hills from the east, we can drive in and perhaps outflank him. I propose that we proceed from here to the main stage road, at Rebosadero Springs." He tapped a forefinger on the map. "It may be that we will encounter him or at least discover his line of march."

Baylor nodded and looked at Gillett, standing next to him. "Sergeant, do you have any thoughts?"

"This seems reasonable to me, Lieutenant."

"Very well, then," Terrazas said. "Let us tell our men to prepare for the march."

Carrizal, Chihuahua State, Mexico
October 4, 1880

Dear Annie,

Well, it looks like we are preparing to ride out once more into the Mexican desert, hunting for Victorio and his renegade Apaches. I wish that I could sort out all the thoughts and feelings I have about this prospect. As a loyal American, I suppose I should be all for his forcible return to the reservation or, failing that, his death. He has killed many people on both sides of the Rio Grande, many of them innocent of any insult to him or his people.

And yet, I confess that my mind is not easy on this matter. Annie, I cannot fully express myself to any of my associates hereabout, not even Jim, who is more understanding than most. Only when I write to you am I able to truly reveal the conflict that rages in my breast when I contemplate what I consider to be the fundamental unfairness—no, call it what it truly is—the injustice being inflicted on Victorio and his people by the government of the United States and its counterpart in Mexico.

Here is a man whose only desire is to continue to live as his ancestors have lived for untold years into the past. And yet, because we "white eyes"—for that is what he calls us, and it is a name better than we deserve of him, I think—because we want the lands of his ancestors, we therefore believe we should have them, and he should not. And his reward for resisting our aims? We force him onto a piece of land where nothing resembles his accustomed surroundings and wonder why he has the ingratitude to leave it, then to fight us in order to remain in a place of his own choosing.

But, my dear Annie, when I say such things to the men all around me—indeed, it seems to me, when I even think along such lines—I am regarded as a traitor of some sort. It is a lamentable predicament in which I find myself. I can be no less than true to my chosen comrades, to defend their honest and upright lives with my own. And at the same time, we are engaged upon a course that, when I am most honest with myself, I regard as despicable.

I beg you, Annie, if you are indeed reading these words, as I hope, do not show this letter to anyone. I do not think there is anyone in the wide creation who could possibly understand the conflict I feel within myself. Indeed, I sometimes wonder if the reason I have no replies from you is because you see me for the pitiful creature that I am, "forever limping back and forth between two opinions," as Scripture says. I hope that you can think better of me.

I wish very much to come back to Colorado and once again see that face that so delighted me in the show at the Orpheum in Denver. How I loved the sound of your singing! Sometimes when we are on a long, hot ride, or when we are lying down to sleep around a dying campfire, I try to remember every note of the last song I heard you sing, back before Andrews and I left Colorado to try to make our fortunes in Texas. But I have only a poor ear for music, and except for the memories of you it summons, the exercise does me no good.

Oh, Annie, please think as kindly of me as you can! One day I will come back to the north country and hear once again that voice that I treasure above all others, though I experienced it for all too short a time.

Until then, I remain,
as ever,
your most faithful admirer,

William Wiswall

Wiswall read the letter from beginning to end one more time. With a deep sigh, he folded it and placed it in the envelope. He addressed it to Miss Annie Milligan, in care of the Tabor Opera House, Leadville, Colorado.

When would he even be able to mail the letter? And would this one have any better success at reaching its intended recipient than the others that had preceded it? Or—as he hated to think, even though he could not help himself—had all his letters arrived, only to be discarded by a woman who had no wish to receive his attentions, even through the mail?

Sometimes Wiswall thought he would have written the letters, even if he knew they would never be read. In some way he didn't fully understand, as he wrote to Annie, he was able to get the tangled thoughts out of his head and onto the foolscap. He found a sort of relief in the exercise.

Maybe I ought to just keep a journal, he thought. It would do just as well, perhaps.

But, no. It was the image of Annie on the stage, the memory of her voice, her smile, the few minutes they had spent together on that night after her performance at the Denver Orpheum, the look in her eye that, he fancied, held something more than polite interest. The thought of her pulled him forward, gave an object to his contemplation and his wish to fully bear witness to the conflict in his soul. The notion, however remote the possibility, that she might actually read his words made the difference. It tipped the balance.

He heard Andrews' long-legged stride crossing the wooden floor of the house where the Rangers were headquartered.

"Time to saddle up, partner," Andrews said. "We've gotten our orders."

Wiswall looked at the address on his envelope for several seconds. He brushed it gently with a forefinger, and then he slid the envelope into his saddlebag.

Chapter 15

The young man shook his head wearily. "They are already there, Bidu-ya. If we go any nearer to the pass, the bluecoats will surely know we are here and will attack us."

"Then we will have to go around," Victorio said. "We have little ammunition, so we cannot fight them. And our horses are too tired to run away from them. The bluecoats must not know we are here."

As the men swung back onto their ponies, Victorio looked up at the sun and peered away toward the southwest. He had been hoping against hope that they would be able to use Borracho Pass; the easier going would have saved them several hours. The horses badly needed water, and every day he was away from Nana and the women and children was another day he was unable to protect his people—his granddaughter.

Maybe they could make it to the place called Lagunita before darkness came. There was usually some water there. Even one night of rest and a good drink for the horses would be a great help. Close to Lagunita, the Sierra de los Piños offered them a place where they could more easily travel without being detected or tracked. They could follow the mountains down to the Castillo Plain, where his people waited in the shadow of the three huge rock formations the Mexicans called Tres Castillos.

Once again, Victorio remembered the old creation story, when Child of the Water, the son of White Painted Woman, had killed the monsters from each of the four cardinal points of the compass. With his victory over the monsters that roamed the world Usen had created, Child of the Water made it safe for human beings to come out of hiding, to hunt and eat, to dance and tell stories.

But now, the monsters had come again. The Chihenne were once more surrounded by enemies who wanted to make them prisoners and kill them, and unlike Child of the Water, Victorio had no arrows with powerful medicine to use in slaying them. The blue-coats guarded the passes and watering places between here and the big river, and they guarded those across the river, as well. The Mexicans, aided by the Texas Rangers, were on his trail, no matter where he led his people. Only by the barest luck had they been able to steal away from their camp in the Candelarias without being seen by the arriving bluecoats.

He reined his pony along the shoulder of the rocky slope, and his men came along behind. They moved quietly, without talking, and the ponies walked with their heads down, too fatigued and thirsty to do any-thing except watch their feet in the rough terrain.

Victorio's eyes roved the landscape, and his ears were attuned to the surroundings, alert for any sound that was out of place. But even as he kept watch, he prayed to Usen for one more day, one more place where they could get water, one more night of rest that would bring them closer to the place where the rest of his people waited.

On the second day after the arrival of the joint force at Rebosadero Springs, a party of Navajo scouts reported to General Terrazas and Lieutenant Baylor that they had thoroughly reconnoitered the Candelarias, but Victorio was not to be found.

"There are many bluecoats there," one of the men told the two commanders. "They have crossed into Mexico just northeast of Los Juguetes," the scout said. "They are led by one named Buell."

Baylor nodded. "That will be General Buell, from Fort Cummings." With his finger, he traced a line on the map from just north of the New Mexico line down to the Candelarias. "It's too bad we couldn't have gotten here before Victorio hightailed it," he said. "With Buell's forces coming down from the northwest, here, we could have closed in from this side and caught Victorio between a hammer and an anvil."

Terrazas stroked his chin. "However, I do not believe we are in that situation now, Lieutenant." He studied the map a few seconds, and then said, "If he is no longer here, then we must assume he is moving east, away from General Buell's forces. I then believe we should proceed here, to Borracho Pass."

"He used that as a campsite the last time he crossed the river from Texas," Baylor said. "Right after he raided Jesus Cota's rancho."

Terrazas nodded decisively. "Then it may be that he will go there again." He looked at Baylor. "How soon can your men be ready to leave?"

Baylor shrugged. "Before dark, if you like, General."

"No, that will not be necessary, I think," Terrazas said. "In the morning, then."

"As you wish, General."

Andrews sat up on his bedroll and tried to blink the sleep out of his eyes. Dawn pinked the eastern sky. Shep stood beside him, his nose inches from Andrews's face.

"Well, dammit, pooch, if you're in such a gol-danged hurry to break camp, why didn't you make some coffee?" Andrews said, running a hand through his hair. "That would have saved some time."

Wiswall sat up and yawned. "Never mind him, Shep. You know he's always a sorehead in the mornings."

Shep sat on his haunches, but his eyes never left Andrews. "You know something is up, don't you, old fellow?" Andrews said. A sleepy grin stole across his face. "You always know."

Wiswall reached for his boots, sitting on the low adobe wall beside the place he had slept. "I hear we're riding east. Looks like Victorio has cleared out of the Candelarias, lock, stock, and barrel." He turned his boots upside down, banged them on the wall a few times, and began to pull them on.

Andrews searched around, bleary-eyed, until he saw his hat. He picked it up, peered inside, whacked it on the ground a few times, looked inside one more time, and settled it on his head. Andrews pulled on his boots and levered himself upright. He quickly rolled up his blankets and stuffed them in the crook of a nearby mesquite. He stepped behind the tree and emptied his bladder. "I wonder if the sergeant has the coffee pot on yet? Reckon I'll go see."

"Send the valet to my room, would you?" Wiswall said to Andrews' departing back. He looked over at Shep, whose unflinching gaze had now shifted from Andrews to Wiswall, still seated on his bedroll.

"All right, all right. I'm getting up." Wiswall got his feet under him and raised himself to stand on the ground beside his blankets. He spread his hands and gave Shep a little bow. "See?" He shook out his blankets and rolled them up, then tied the ends with rawhide strings. Setting his bedroll atop the adobe wall, he yawned and stretched.

With Shep padding beside him, he went to the corral where the horses of the Rangers and their Mexican volunteers were kept. He scooped a handful of oats from a hogshead standing beside the ramshackle shed near the horse pen, then let himself inside. He walked slowly among the horses until he saw his mount, a chestnut gelding with a white stocking on his off back foot; the Rangers called him Gus.

"Here you go, fellow," Wiswall said in a low voice, moving up slowly beside Gus and putting one arm over the horse's neck as he offered the oats in the open palm of his other hand. He felt the velvet-and-leather of the gelding's lips as he nuzzled the grain from his palm. Wiswall patted the gelding down, murmuring softly as he went, looking for any untreated cuts or anything else about his mount that might need attention before the day's ride. He looped the rope he had brought loosely around Gus's neck and led him toward the corral gate, where Shep waited patiently.

The rickety shed held the Rangers' tack. Wiswall found his bridle, slid it over Gus's ears, and guided the bit between his teeth before buckling the chin strap. He grabbed the braided saddle blanket and used it to rub the horse's back before settling it gently and evenly, just behind the gelding's withers. He grabbed his saddle with both hands and, with a little grunt, plopped it down on top of the saddle blanket. He reached beneath Gus's belly to grab the front latigo strap and pull it tight through the ring on the front cinch. He tied off the strap and then did the same for the rear strap.

"All right, Gus, let's go get you another drink. It's liable to be a long, dry day." He led the gelding out of the shed and over to the water trough beside the corral. Gus drank in deep slurps, then pulled his snout, dripping, from the trough and leaned down to touch noses with Shep, who was standing beside him.

"Do you reckon that today is the day we'll find him, Shep?" Wiswall said, staring off toward the east, the general direction of today's ride. "We've been chasing him for so long, sometimes I forget that one of these days, we may actually catch up with him."

Standing face to face on the plain at Crow Flat,with Shep at his side, Wiswall had told Victorio that loyalty was a thing worth dying for. And for some reason, after hearing these words, Victorio had decided to let him and the rest of his companions ride away alive. He didn't think there was much chance of General Terrazas returning that particular favor.

He looked down at Shep. The dog's head was turned, like his, toward the east. His nostrils worked in and out, testing the air.

"Well, I guess you're right," Wiswall said, leaning down to ruffle the back of Shep's neck. "Wherever we're headed, it's time to get started going there."

Chapter 16

Though the morning had admitted a hint of the coming cool of autumn, by midafternoon the heat had climbed back onto everyone's shoulders. The men, the horses, and the mules all had their heads down, just plodding along in the brown, baking country. Even the cenizo and the escobilla looked to Andrews as though they were sick to death of the endless summer, ready for anything that would relieve the constant burden of the sun.

They rode in a long column across the gypsum flats and the flinty plain, crossed here and there by the dry, scrub-lined wash of a seasonal stream. General Terrazas and his cavalry were in the lead, followed by the Tarahumara infantry. Baylor and his Rangers, augmented by the Mexican volunteers, guarded the column's rear.

Shep seemed impatient with having to follow the Mexican troops, yet he clearly did not wish to be so far separated from Andrews and Wiswall that he could not easily locate them whenever he wanted to. He would alternately range ahead, then pause, seeming to remember himself as he looked back along the line of riders and walkers to where his human partners rode with their fellows. The very outline of reluctance, he would then turn and trot slowly back until he had satisfied himself with his position relative to them, before resuming the march.

The Tarahumara were proving every bit as durable as Andrews and Wiswall had been led to believe. Only rarely might one observe one of the foot soldiers taking a brief sip of water; otherwise, they seemed the human equivalent of the camels in the Arabian desert.

An hour or two past noon, a halt worked its way back from the front of the formation. Baylor sent Gillett up to find out the cause, and the sergeant soon cantered back to tell his lieutenant that the scouts had encountered fresh sign. "They think Victorio might be close, but they can't tell for sure."

Baylor unfolded his map. He studied it for a moment, now and then glancing at the position of the sun. "I make us about halfway between Rebosadero and Borracho Pass." He thought a moment, then turned to Aniceto. "Go and talk to the other scouts. You've trailed Victorio and his people as much as any of them; see what you think, and then come back and tell me."

The Tigua reined his horse away from the Rangers and urged it into a quick trot toward the van. But before Aniceto could return, one of Terrazas's cavalry officers rode up to ask the lieutenant and sergeant to join the general in a quick council.

"Unlimber your weapons," Baylor said when he rode back, a half-hour later. "If Victorio isn't about, he has been, and not long since. We're in fairly open country now, but as we approach the broken country around Borracho Pass, we'll be entering Vic's favorite ambush terrain. Keep your eyes open."

For the rest of that long, hot afternoon, they rode with their rifles resting on their saddle horns, fingers through the trigger guard. Their eyes roved back and forth across the brown, dusty surroundings. Wiswall realized that he fancied movement behind every cholla, a pair of Apache eyes peering from behind every prickly pear outcropping.

"Just keep an eye on Shep," Andrews said. "He'll let us know if anything is amiss."

"As long as the Apaches don't pick him off first," Wiswall said.

Andrews looked at him with an odd expression. "Do you really think that's likely, after what we've seen?"

Wiswall shrugged. "I reckon not. Heat must be making me soft in the head."

Andrews nodded knowingly. "Take a little drink. Keep riding."

The country started to break apart in ravines that cut through the hillsides rising in front of them. A couple of hours before sundown, Terrazas called another halt to allow the Indian scouts to work their way up along the rims and canyon walls, searching for any sign of an ambush. Just as the bottom edge of the sun touched the western horizon, the all-clear came, and the column rode along the trail that soon brought them to Borracho Pass and the small, green alcove in the bend of a stream bed where they would camp.

"The general says we'll wait here for the supply wagons to come from El Carrera and Carrizal," Baylor announced to his men as they pulled the saddles from their weary horses and began unpacking the foodstuffs from the mule packs. They watered the horses and mules from the filled goatskins they had brought from Carrizal and built their cooking fires in the middle of small clearings in the scrub mesquite and shin oak that clustered in their camping place.

As dark came on, the air grew cooler, which was a small relief. But the wash was dry, and there was no spring, so they would need to continue to carefully nurse their water until the supply train reached them.

"Just enough water to make the biscuits and tortillas," Sergeant Gillett announced, "and maybe a pot or two of coffee. Let's hold off on boiling beans until we get re-supplied."

"All right, sergeant," one of the men said, "but if I have to keep a-chawin' this damned old jerky much longer, I'm fixing to start eating my saddle."

Propping his saddle against a mesquite trunk and leaning his back against it as he sat on the ground, Wiswall fished the letter to Annie out of his saddlebag. He looked at it for a few seconds, then flicked open the flap of the envelope and unfolded the letter.

"No post office hereabout," Andrews said, coming up behind him.

Wiswall quickly folded the letter and stuffed it back in the envelope. He stared ahead into the darkness, his cheeks stinging with embarrassment.

"Want this?" Andrews said, holding a steaming cup of coffee toward him.

"Much obliged," Wiswall said, taking the tin cup and taking a careful sip.

"You calculate to go find her." Andrews said after a long silence.

Wiswall took another sip of coffee and stared for a while into the night. "I don't know. I expect you think I'm a fool."

"Not a bit. Hell, she's a fine-looking woman. I josh you about it, but that's just my way. You know that."

Wiswall nodded. He stared at the coffee in his cup. "I don't know which would be worse—not finding her, or finding her and realizing she threw all my letters away because I was just another lonesome drifter."

Andrews took a slow sip from his cup. After about a minute, he said, "Well, I don't imagine you'll be ready to head out to south California until you know, one way or the other."

Wiswall looked at his partner. "You'd give me the time to do that?"

Andrews gave him a slow smile. "You think I have a choice in the matter?"

Wiswall ducked his head. "Well," he said after a while, "I appreciate it."

They sat in camp all the next day, moving about only as much as necessary to tend to the hobbled horses or to prepare their next meal. Some of the men allowed that the weather seemed a little cooler, the farther into October they went and the closer they approached the higher country around the Sierras de los Piños.

One of the Mexican volunteers brought down a deer in one of the surrounding ravines, which earned him a lecture from one of Terrazas's cavalry officers for firing a weapon unnecessarily.

"As if Victorio didn't already know exactly where we are," Sergeant Gillett said. "Still, I guess it is probably best to make as little disturbance as we can."

They butchered the deer and roasted venison steaks over the coals that evening. They cut up the rest of the meat, intending to make a stew of it, combined with some beans, when they had enough water to spare.

Just before noon of the next day, they heard the sound of harness and hooves, and soon three wagons, drawn by sturdy little Mexican mules, pulled into the campsite. General Terrazas sent word to Baylor that he should have his Rangers and volunteers come and draw ten days' rations from the store. Soon, a throng of men gathered around the wagons, waiting in the sun for their chance to carry away salt-cured bacon, corn meal, coffee, beans, and rice. There were even a few sacks of dried apples, but these were gone before even half of the men had received their allotments.

Gillett came back from the wagons complaining of the loss of his belt knife. "I was standing with the others, and suddenly I realized my knife was gone," he said. "It's a damned shame, too, if you'll pardon me. I've carried that hunting knife since I came out west from Menard. I'm pretty sure that one of the general's men lifted it off of me in the crush around the commissary wagons."

Baylor promised his sergeant that he would communicate the loss to General Terrazas. Upon learning of the incident, Terrazas ordered his officers to search their men, but the culprit was not found and the knife remained lost, much to Gillett's disgust.

"Like as not, the rascal tossed it under a cactus when the search order came," Gillett said. "I expect I've lost my knife for good."

Toward evening of that day, the sentinels reported an approaching band of horsemen, all well armed. This soon proved to be a company of the Ninth US Cavalry, a column of Buffalo Soldiers led by a Lieutenant Charles Schaeffer.

"General Buell sends his regards," the lieutenant said to General Terrazas, after giving a smart salute. "We have been following his trail since the Candelarias, and we have left men at every water hole and spring of any size. He will not be found anywhere between here and the border with New Mexico."

"That is good news, Lieutenant," Terrazas said. "With your general's help, we are tightening the noose. Soon we will run Victorio to ground."

"Our Chiricahua scouts tell us that he is not leaving trail sign," Schaeffer went on. "Whatever band we are following, it travels alone, communicating with no one else."

Terrazas nodded. "It may be that he is trying to reach his main band, somewhere ahead of us." He requested a map from an aide and studied it for a few seconds. "It may also be that we will come upon them soon." Terrazas looked up at the lieutenant. "And when we do, we will show them no mercy."

Chapter 17

When Victorio saw the long series of sand dunes, he knew that at last, they were nearly arrived at Tres Castillos. It was good; the ponies were desperately tired, after the hard trail down the spine of the Sierra de los Piños, with little water along the way.

Just as they came down the southern shoulders of the range, though, they had chanced upon a small herd of cattle grazing at the edge of the Llano de los Castillos. Only one herdsman was with the animals, and when he saw how many warriors he faced, he rode away as fast as he could. Victorio and his fighters had rounded up the cattle and driven them along as they continued toward the camp. They could be butchered to supply extra meat for the long trek westward to Juh in the Blue Mountains.

Nana greeted them at the edge of the camp. Rains had come through a few days before, he told them, and the grass around the small lake was good. Waterfowl could be taken, and their eggs could be gathered. The people had been able to rest, he said, and after the warrior band had a chance to recover from their hard ride, they would be able to start toward the Blue Mountains with full bellies and skins full of water.

Victorio was glad. For the first time in many days, he felt something like hope. His people had been driven to the edge of desperation, but now there was a way forward. Juh's lands were far from the Warm Springs country of Victorio's homeland, but at least in the Blue Mountains they would be safe. They could rest and grow stronger, and perhaps one day, they might be able to return to the place Usen had given them when all things were made.

When he slid off his pony, Liluye ran toward him, her arms out. He scooped up his granddaughter and held her close. "My heart sings like the hawk to see you, little one," he whispered in her ear.

"You always say that, Grandfather," she giggled.

"You are Liluye—Hawk Singing—what else should I say?" he said, a weary smile on his face.

"I do not get tired of hearing it," she said, her arms clasped around his neck. "I am glad that you and the other men have come back to us."

"Have you been busy, helping Onawa prepare for the long journey?" he said, setting her astride his pony. "Have you been helping to cut the strips of meat for drying, as I told you?"

"Yes, Grandfather." She toyed with the pony's mane as Victorio led his horse toward the edge of the lake. "And I have cut the hides into strips to make laces, so that we can tie up the packs for carrying. Old Bina says that my hands are the surest of any of the children."

"It is good, little one," Victorio said. "We have a long way to go, and we must travel quickly, to stay ahead of our enemies. We will need packs with good laces."

They reached the edge of the lake, and he helped her slide down from the pony. They watched the horse drink for a few moments and then Liluye said, in a very quiet voice, "Are we safe from the whites now, Grandfather?"

"Not yet, little one," he said. "But soon. We will rest here for a few days, and then we will go to a safe place."

That night Victorio and the other warriors ate the first freshly cooked meat they had had in many days. He had almost forgotten how good the smoke from the cooking fire smelled as the fat dripped down and sizzled on the coals. The women had dug a fire pit, and along with the beef and duck, they had roasted mescal. The sweet, pithy hearts of the mescal tasted good after so many days of eating only trail rations.

After the meal, Victorio gathered his leaders around the fire. "The brown coats are on our trail," he said. "We have only a few days here before they reach us, but no more. We must be ready to move, and we must get to Juh's territory as soon as we can. It is our only chance."

"The men we sent out to get ammunition have not come back," Nana said. "I do not know what has happened to them."

"It does not matter now," Victorio said. "We cannot wait for them. For now, we will have to run instead of fighting."

"We found many cached hides here when we arrived," Nana said. "There were jars of corn. And there were points for arrows, and a little ammunition, but not much."

Victorio nodded. "It is good. Tell the women to butcher the cattle we have brought and to dry as much of the meat as they can. Whatever we cannot eat or dry in the next few days, we must leave behind. Give the horses as much rest and water as possible. It is a long way across to the Blue Mountains, and we must go around the towns of the Mexicans."

That night, Victorio lay on the cool grass beside the lake. He pulled his sleeping robe over his chest and lay with his arm behind his head, looking up at the night sky, dusted with stars.

Maybe they would be able to escape. Maybe Liluye would be able to grow up free, breathing the mountain air instead living on that foul patch of desert at San Carlos. Maybe once again the old men would carve the *tsoch* for the babies and the young boys and girls would be properly taught the ways of the Chihenne. They would learn the stories of White Painted Woman, Killer of Enemies, and Child of the Water. They would live in the way that Usen meant for the *nideh*.

He closed his eyes. Tonight, others eyes could watch, other ears could listen. The breeze brushed his face, and somewhere in the darkness he heard the call of a hunting owl. He slept.

A day out of Borracho Pass, the scouts discovered the traces of a camp Victorio had used on his path to the south. They studied the ground and reconstructed for General Terrazas, Lieutenant Baylor, and Lieutenant Schaeffer where the Apaches' ponies had been tethered, where the cooking fire had been, and approximately how many men had slept there. They had watered their horses and then ridden up into the Sierra de los Piños, in accordance with the Apaches' penchant for keeping to the high country, where they were more difficult to track.

But track them the scouts did, leading the combined Mexican and American forces deeper and deeper into the Los Piños range. Terrazas deployed the supply wagons, accompanied by most of his cavalry, in the passes, while Baylor's Rangers rode with him along the ridges and slopes, accompanied by the tireless Tarahumaras.

Wiswall watched the Indian foot soldiers, treading for hour after hour across the rock-strewn inclines and leaping the crevasses as they followed the trail the scouts traced. They wore rope sandals—or they went barefooted; it appeared to matter little to them. Now and then they sipped a little water from the skins they carried.

One day, as the patrol bivouacked in the scant shade of some piñon pines lining a narrow ravine, Wiswall found himself next to one of the Tarahumaras. The man came from a place called Huejotitán, a seven-day walk south of Chihuahua City, he said. At least, with Wiswall's poor Spanish, that was what he thought the man said.

Wiswall wanted to know what motivated the Tarahumaras to fight against Victorio. "*¿Por qué lucha contra Victorio y sus gentes?*" he said in his halting Spanish.

"*Los Apaches nos matan,*" the foot soldier said. "They kill us and take our cattle, our goats. With *el ejército y* Terrazas, maybe we protect our people."

Wiswall nodded. The Tarahumara looked at him. "*Pero, cuando los Apaches se han ido*—when Apache is gone—who protects Tarahumaras from army?"

Wiswall shook his head. "*No sé, amigo.* I don't know."

The other man gave him a sad smile and shrugged. "*¿Quién sabe?* That is a problem for another day."

Three days later, they found another abandoned camp in a small box canyon near the southern edge of the mountain range.

"The trail continues south," Terrazas told the other commanders. "I think he is going to Tres Castillos."

Chapter 18

By the time they began descending the southern flanks of the Sierra de los Piños, the weather had finally begun to cool. Even as they came down from the higher elevations and neared the broad expanse of the Llano de los Castillos, the days had relinquished most of their punishing heat.

"About damned time," Andrews commented. "We're nearly to the middle of October."

On the morning after the first night they camped at the edge of the plain, Aniceto Duran reported to Lieutenant Baylor that he and one of the Navajo scouts had seen the glow of fires, far away on the southern reaches of the plain. "Victorio," he assured the Ranger commander. "He camps with his people."

In response to this intelligence, General Terrazas deployed his forces carefully around the plain of Tres Castillos; he sent half of the infantry, accompanied by an escort of thirty cavalry, far around to the western side of the plain, with orders not to engage Victorio, but to prevent any movement to the west, should he attempt it. Next, he ordered the rest of the Tarahumara foot soldiers toward the east side of the desolate plain, with similar orders to contain any movement to the east.

"Looks like Vic is bottled up, whether he realizes it or not," Sergeant Gillett said as he, along with the other Rangers, watched the infantry move out to take up the positions from which the final attack on Victorio would be launched. "I calculate that the rest of Terrazas's horse, along with the army boys and us, will ride in on him from here. It'll take some pretty fancy footwork for him to get out of this situation."

"Well, I wish we could get on with it, then," said one of the other men. "I believe I've enjoyed about all I can stand of riding through the Mexican desert and sleeping on top of cholla cactus. I'm ready to head back to Ysleta."

Wiswall watched the departing troops, then peered south toward the place, a few miles across the plain, where the three rock formations abruptly rose like strange, haphazard castles, giving the place its name. He tried to imagine what might be going through Victorio's mind. The old chief had successfully evaded the Rangers and the armies of the United States and Mexico for more than a year now; it was hard to believe that he had no inkling of the forces now moving to surround him. When Terrazas sprang his trap, would he find his fox already fled, as the crafty Apache had done so many times before? Or was this the time that Victorio really was cornered, with nowhere left to run?

Shep sat on his haunches studying the marching infantry and their cavalry escorts as carefully as a general on a reviewing stand. Wiswall leaned over and scratched the dog behind his ears and along his neck. "What do you think, old boy? Will they get him this time?" He realized that he was not including himself among the number involved in finishing the fight with Victorio. He couldn't explain it to himself, but he let it be. He might be with the others, but he didn't share their mission. Not exactly.

Near sundown, Baylor and Lieutenant Schaeffer were summoned to a council at General Terrazas's tent. They were gone for an hour, and when they returned, Wiswall could tell immediately that something unexpected had transpired. Baylor looked like a man who just realized he had eaten a piece of bad pork. He called the Rangers together.

"Men, at sunup, we ride back to Texas."

Uncomprehending stares greeted this pronouncement.

"This comes straight from General Terrazas. For some reason, the Mexicans suddenly don't want us—or the army either—this deep in their country. Lieutenant Schaeffer and I have been politely but firmly requested to turn ourselves around and go back to the north side of the Rio Grande."

"The son of a bitch doesn't want to share the credit," one of the men muttered from the side of his mouth.

"When does Terrazas intend to attack Victorio's camp?" Sergeant Gillett asked.

"From all indications, he will attack either tomorrow or the next day, at dawn."

"Well, I'll be damned," someone said.

"I know it's disappointing," the lieutenant said. "We've been chasing Victorio on both sides of the river, for nearly a year now. But it doesn't appear to me that we have any choice in the matter. I don't think President Hayes would care for us starting a war with Mexico, not to mention that we would be outgunned. And that's before we ever got to where Victorio waits."

"What about the volunteers who have been riding with us?" Andrews asked.

"They are Mexican nationals. They will remain with the general and his forces." Baylor looked around at the ring of stony, silent faces. "Men, I hope you understand that I don't like this any better than you do. I'm accustomed to finishing a mission, no matter how difficult it is or how long it takes. But we came here as invited guests of the Mexican government, and that invitation has just been revoked. We have no choice about this."

There were a few heavy sighs; someone in the back of the group loudly spat a stream of tobacco juice into the dust.

"Eat some grub and get a good night's sleep; we'll ride out at first light," Baylor said. "You are dismissed."

Wiswall felt a strange sense of relief as he and Andrews walked toward the cooking fire. *At least I won't have to be the one who kills him,* he thought. Though the final outcome for Victorio and his people wouldn't likely be improved by the circumstances, at least he would not have to participate in or witness the violent end of a man who, he had to reluctantly admit to himself, had earned his respect.

"Well, do you reckon this moves up your departure for the opera houses and salons of Colorado?" Andrews said as they held out their plates for a ladle full of beans from the cast iron pot.

"Maybe," Wiswall said. "And maybe we'll get to south California before the weather gets too cold."

"That would be a mercy," Andrews said. "Though what we'll use for money when we get there is unclear to me."

The general belief of the Rangers, mostly glum-faced as they spooned their beans and chomped their biscuits, was that the supposed concern of the Mexican government for foreign troops on their soil was largely a fabrication of the general, created to justify his desire to garner all the credit for vanquishing the troublesome Victorio.

"I don't reckon *El Presidente* Diaz knows or gives half a damn about this here little adventure of ours," one of the men said. "I calculate that old Terrazas is using him as an excuse to get us out of the way."

"Hell, I expect they'll make him governor of Chihuahua after this," another Ranger said. "His cousin already is; they're all in cahoots."

In the gathering dark, Wiswall leaned back against his saddle and stared at the envelope in his hand, addressed to Annie's last suspected whereabouts. He ran his finger slowly along the edge of the envelope. He thumbed open the flap and took out his letter, re-reading it slowly.

"You'll find her," Andrews said, coming to sit beside Wiswall. "I've got a good feeling about it."

Wiswall shrugged, folding the letter and sliding it back into the envelope. "Musicians move around a lot, I expect," he said. "Especially in Colorado. At least, that's what the sheriff in Leadville told me, when he answered my last inquiry." He turned around to tuck the letter back into his saddlebag, then peered up at the purple evening sky. "Still, I sure hope your feeling is correct."

Andrews nodded.

One of the other Rangers approached. "Hey, boys, where's that dog of yours?" He held up a bone with a palm-sized piece of gristly meat still attached. "This was in the bottom of the bean pot, and they were fixing to toss it into the weeds. I figured ol' Shep might enjoy it."

"Much obliged," Wiswall said, getting to his feet and dusting the seat of his pants. "I'll take it. He's most likely over by the Mexicans' campfire, angling for an extra tamale or two." He took the bone and, accompanied by Andrews, wandered in the general direction of the volunteers' part of the campsite.

But Shep wasn't there. He also wasn't around Terrazas's tent or with the Buffalo Soldiers who rode with Lieutenant Schaeffer.

"This isn't like him," Andrews said, as man after man shook his head and said, in English or Spanish, that the dog hadn't been seen lately. "Come to think of it, I can't remember the last time he went more than an hour or two without checking in on one of the two of us."

Wiswall stared around into the growing darkness, telling himself to master the alarm that was building in his imagination. He looked at Andrews. "I think I know where he is—or, at least, where he's headed."

Andrews stared at him. "Lord a'mighty. You really think so?"

Wiswall nodded. "He's gone to see Victorio. One last time."

Andrews took a deep breath and let it puff out his cheeks. "Well," he said after a while, "I guess we'd better saddle up—pretty damned quietly."

"You don't have to go," Wiswall said quickly. "Victorio will remember me from Crow Flat. I can probably get in and out by myself."

"The hell you say," Andrews said. "I'm not riding back towards Texas without that dog—or you."

A quiet footfall made them both turn. It was Aniceto Duran. The Tigua looked at both of them for several seconds, then said, "I will take you to the dog. To Victorio."

Wiswall and Andrews stared, slack-jawed, at the scout.

"But we must leave very soon," Aniceto said. "I will

meet you in the small *cañon* behind the general's tent."
He turned and faded into the night.

Wiswall and Andrews looked at each other for a
few seconds, and then they headed toward where the
horses were tethered.

As he walked, Wiswall realized he was still carrying the bone. *Oh, well, might as well bring it, he thought.*
One last treat for old Shep . . .

Chapter 19

The dog ran along the flinty soil in the darkness. He had never been here before, but he knew where he was going. The man with the sad eyes was out there, somewhere ahead of him in the night, and the dog had to reach him. He had to see the man one more time, and this would be his only chance. After tonight, the dog sensed, the man with the sad eyes would not be anywhere that the dog could go.

The dog was troubled by running away from the two men who always fed him—the tall one and the stocky one who talked to him the most. But he would go back to the men, once he had seen the sad-eyed man and sniffed his skin, one last time.

The dog loped along, his ears and nose on full alert, and his eyes gathering in what little light remained as the stars winked into view. He had to be careful about stepping in one of the holes inhabited by the rattlesnakes, with their venomous fangs. He had to avoid the spiny prickly pear, the fierce catclaw mimosa with its vicious, recurved thorns.

But most of all, he had to reach the man with the sad eyes, the one who looked at him and knew who he was. The dog did not want anything bad to happen to the man, but from the voices of the other men who rode the horses, he could tell. The way they kept looking toward the place where the sad-eyed man waited told the dog that they knew where he was and that they meant to go and fight him.

There would be pain, blood, and death. The dog needed to reach the man with the sad eyes before that happened. This was his last chance. And so he ran on, deeper and deeper into the desert—deeper and deeper into the night.

Andrews and Wiswall rode one behind the other, both of them following the dim figure of Aniceto Duran, moving steadily along in front of them. They did not know if he was somehow trailing Shep as he raced toward Victorio's camp, or if he simply knew the way— even though he had never been there before. They only knew that if they followed Aniceto, they would end up where they meant to go.

They spoke very little, and then in the lowest voices possible. Once, Andrews asked Wiswall if they might not get themselves shot, deserting the Rangers this way.

"We aren't deserting, Andrews. You know that as well as I do. We'll either be back here by morning, or we'll be dead. But we're not running away."

Neither of them said anything else for a long time. But the air around their heads was thick with imaginings about what might happen in the next few hours. They both kept fingering their rifles, holstered beneath their legs as they rode, then withdrawing their hands. If it came to fighting, they had very little chance of coming out alive, and they knew that. But they weren't riding to Victorio's camp to fight. They were riding there because of Shep.

Damned dog, Wiswall thought for about the hundredth time in the last five minutes. *If I could talk hound, I'd give him a piece of my mind, sure enough.* If they caught up to him. And if Victorio or one of his lookouts didn't kill them first.

The night air was chilly. Wiswall tugged the collar of his duster closer around his throat. He wondered how much farther they had to go.

Nana was the first one to see the silent shape, slipping along among the boulders scattered at the base of one of the three upthrust granite promontories. Sitting beside Victorio, he touched the chief's arm and pointed.

"It is the brother of Coyote," Victorio breathed. He felt his heart freezing within him. There could be only one reason why the dog was here; he had come to warn Victorio that death was drawing near.

The dog, frequently dipping his nose to the ground and then raising his head to test the air, came across the rock-strewn ground to where Victorio and Nana sat. He walked straight up to Victorio and looked the chief directly in the eye.

For a long time, nothing moved. To Victorio, it seemed that even the night noises of the desert ceased. He stared into the eyes of the brother of Coyote, and what he saw there made him want to weep—or sing a slow song of mourning.

"You have come to tell us about the ending, brother of Coyote," Victorio said at last, reaching a hand to place on top of the dog's head. "You barked to warn us in the canyon on the other side of the big river, and now you have come again to let us know that our enemies are here."

The dog reached toward him with his muzzle. Victorio smiled and rubbed his hand along the side of the animal's neck. He turned to a young man who sat nearby. "Go and get Liluye. I want her to come here." The young man got up and strode away, coming back a minute or two later with the little girl. Liluye was rubbing her eyes.

"I was asleep, Grandfather," she said. "But when Dahkeya called me, I came."

"It is good, Liluye. Come here and stand beside me." The girl noticed the dog. Her eyes fixed on the animal, she stepped slowly to her grandfather's side.

"Brother of Coyote, this is my granddaughter, Liluye. Do you see her?"

The dog turned his muzzle toward the girl. He nudged her arm with his nose, and his tongue flickered out to gently lick the back of her hand.

"Granddaughter, this is the brother of Coyote. He comes to warn us of danger."

Liluye's eyes flickered from her grandfather to the dog.

"Brother of Coyote, I ask a favor from you. I ask you to protect this child. Watch over her with your cunning. Guard her with your faithfulness. Will you do this for me, brother of Coyote?"

The dog turned to look full in Victorio's face. He held this pose for the space of five breaths, then turned back toward the girl.

"Nana, take Liluye, Kaytennae, and a few others. Leave here at once."

The old chief's eyes narrowed. "What have you seen?"

"They are coming, Nana. I do not think I will ride away from this place. But you must go. Some of us can get away."

"Grandfather, I do not want to leave you," Liluye said, her eyes wide. "Do not make me."

Victorio held out his hand to her. She put her small

hand in his large, hard palm. "My child, your way does not end here. The brother of Coyote has shown me that you will find a safe place, a place you can rest."

"But . . . where?"

"I do not know. But I know that you must leave here—tonight. Now." He turned to Nana. "You must go. Take her. Take the others."

Wiswall, Andrews, and Aniceto peered over the edge of the boulder, watching the handful of riders as they left the camp. Wiswall's head was full of questions, but at this distance, he dared not even whisper. He still had no idea how Aniceto had managed to get them this far without being killed or even challenged. For all he knew, one of Victorio's scouts could be crouched within ten feet, ready to send an arrow from the darkness into anyone trying to intrude.

Who was leaving the camp? And why were they so few? If Shep was in there, Victorio had to know that his pursuers were not far behind. Why did he not attempt to get himself and his people to safety, while the night shielded them?

Terrazas had sent troops to encircle this place in order to prevent Victorio's escape, but if he, Andrews, and Aniceto had managed to sneak in this close, what would prevent the wary Apaches from slipping past the Mexican sentinels?

There was a movement off to their left. Wiswall grabbed the grip of his Colt revolver and had it halfway out of the holster when Aniceto put his hand on Wiswall's arm.

"It is the dog," the Tigua guide said in a barely audible voice. "He knows we are here."

His heart pounding in his throat, Wiswall watched as a shape slipped from shadow to shadow, drawing nearer. In a few seconds, he heard the familiar sound of Shep, sniffing the air. The dog padded toward them, his tail wagging slowly.

"Well, I'll be damned," Andrews whispered. "Aniceto was right." He ruffled the fur behind Shep's ears. "You came to see him, didn't you?"

Wiswall looked up. A figure stood over them, silhouetted by the stars. He stood up to face the Apache warrior. "This is our dog," Wiswall said, nodding toward Shep. "We came to get him."

The man didn't move for several seconds. Then, he pointed down the slope, toward the camp.

"We go to talk to Victorio," Aniceto said. "He, too, knows we are here."

With the Apache trailing them, the three men picked their way down the rocky slope toward the bowl-shaped swale that cupped the small *cienega* pond at its center. There were no fires by this time of the night; the only light came from the stars and the glowing coals of a dying cook fire.

Shep went in front of them, making a beeline toward the figure that stood beside the glowing pile of ash and coals.

It was Victorio. His face was indistinct in the starlight, but Wiswall could easily discern the same form that he had faced outside the deserted stage stand—the day when Victorio had allowed them all to ride away because of their faithfulness to this dog. And yet, he was not the same—not exactly. He seemed smaller, worn down.

"Tell him we just came to get our dog, like last time," Andrews said in a low voice to Aniceto.

"You do not need to talk through the Tigua," Victorio said in slow, but clear English. "This time, I speak to you—from my mouth to your ears."

"I spoke to you before," Wiswall said. "Beside the Crow Flat station."

"I see you," Victorio said. "Once again, the brother of Coyote has brought you to me."

Wiswall smiled. "He seems pretty set on getting us together."

"Brother of Coyote has come to bid me a good journey. Tomorrow—or the next day, I do not know when—I will ride the long trail. The one that does not come back this way."

"You can still get away," Wiswall said. "You sent the others to safety; why not follow them?"

Victorio did not answer for a long time. Finally, he shook his head. "I will run no more. I am tired. I do not know the world anymore. Maybe the next world will be a better one."

After a long silence, Wiswall said, "I hope so."

"Take your dog and go back to your people," Victorio said. "One more time, I send you away in safety."

Victorio kneeled down and put his hands on Shep's head. He said some words in the Apache tongue, then stood up. "Goodbye, friends of Coyote. I will see you no more after this."

Chapter 20

Wiswall, Andrews, Aniceto, and Shep arrived back at the Ranger camp about an hour before sunrise. They had just dismounted when one of the men approached. "Lieutenant Baylor asked to see you."

With a glance at each other, Andrews and Wiswall handed their reins to Aniceto. They trudged toward the lieutenant's tent, already being dismantled and packed for the ride back to Ysleta. Shep trailed behind them.

"You asked to see us, Lieutenant?" Andrews said as Baylor turned toward them.

"Yes, James, I did." He looked at them for a long time. "Some of the men noticed you missing, sometime after midnight. I wondered where you might have gotten off to. I was worried about you."

There was a long pause. "We were fine, Lieutenant," Wiswall said. "We just rode out in the country a little ways to pay our respects to someone."

"Oh?" Baylor studied them again for several seconds. "You have a friend in these parts, do you?"

"I wouldn't say a friend—not exactly," Wiswall said. "Someone we know. Someone we don't expect to see again."

Baylor's eyes bored into first Wiswall, then Andrews. The two partners met his gaze steadily. Then he looked down at Shep, standing just behind them. "I guess Shep went with you?"

Andrews gave a tiny smile. "Well, you might say we went with him, Lieutenant. Or went after him, maybe."

Baylor absorbed this with a thoughtful look. "I see." Once again he looked at the two men. "Did you learn anything that should be reported to someone? Say, General Terrazas?"

"No, I don't believe we did," Wiswall said. "Nothing that he doesn't already know, at any rate."

Andrews nodded. "We just paid our respects, and then we came back here—all three of us." He reached behind him and ran the tips of his fingers along the top of Shep's head.

Baylor nodded. "Well. That's all right, then. We ride out for Texas at first light. See to your gear."

"Yes, sir."

Baylor turned away and began tying up the blankets from his bedroll. Andrews and Wiswall went to get their horses back from Aniceto.

"He knows," Andrews said, when they had walked twenty or so paces.

"Of course he knows. And he also knows that nothing we said or did last night made any difference to what's about to take place here. And I, for one, am satisfied as hell to not have to witness it."

In the pink light of dawn, Baylor and his Rangers, accompanied by Lieutenant Schaeffer's Buffalo Soldiers, reined their mounts out of the camp. They were aimed for the Rio Grande, which lay some thirty miles to the north. The Mexican volunteers with whom they had ridden watched them leave; if they had any misgivings about Terrazas's dismissal of their *yanqui* allies, they kept them hidden.

Two days later, as the Ranger column rode along at a leisurely pace through the country just up the river from Fort Quitman, a lone rider on a lathered mount came pounding up from behind them. The Mexican horseman announced in heavily accented English that he bore a message from General Terrazas for *el teniente de los* Rangers.

The day was drawing down toward evening, so Lieutant Baylor called a halt to that day's ride and the men set about making camp. Baylor invited the messenger to share the Rangers' provisions and stay in the camp through the night. "We'll hear your news after we've had some supper and brewed a big pot of coffee," he told the man, who seemed eager to accept the offer.

"I expect I know the tidings we'll hear," Andrews said to Wiswall as they unsaddled their horses and rubbed them down with the saddle blankets.

"Salt in the lieutenant's wound, no doubt," Wiswall said. "He has been chasing Victorio for all this time, and now he's going to learn all about the great victory of *el general grande*. I don't imagine he'll take it too well."

"How will you take it?" Andrews said, giving his friend a thoughtful look.

"You are well acquainted with my views," Wiswall said, after a long pause. "I'm just glad I didn't have to witness it first-hand."

That evening, as the cooling October air pulled the men in close to the campfire, the rider, a vaquero named Carrasco, informed the company that the bold and dangerous Victorio was dead, "killed by General Terrazas *y sus hombres bravos*."

"What a hero," one of the men said from the side of his mouth.

Terrazas had approached Tres Castillos on the day the Rangers and the army rode north, Carrasco told them. He had positioned his men all around the three rocky promontories and posted pickets, planning his attack for the next morning.

During the night, a small party of Apaches had left the camp. Terrazas's forces were able to bring down a couple of them, but about a dozen braves and possibly some women and children got away, Carrasco said.

At dawn, as the Mexican forces advanced upon the Apaches' camp, they were greeted by the sight of Victorio, mounted on a white horse with a rifle gripped in his hands. The warriors were hidden behind the boulders and in fissures of the three stone palisades of Tres Castillos, but the chief seemed to be inviting the attention of his enemies. Terrazas ordered the Tarahumara infantry to open fire, and Victorio fell almost immediately. By noon, the chief and almost ninety warriors lay dead, and nearly that many women and children were taken prisoner. Terrazas lost only two men in the fight, with a few more wounded.

"*El general* is very happy about the defeat of this *muy malo indio*, and he asks me to thank you and your Rangers for your help in bringing Victorio to justice," Carrasco finished.

At this, Wiswall got up and strode off into the darkness. Baylor and the others watched him go; no one said anything. A minute or two later, Shep got up and slinked off in the same direction.

"What will happen to the women and children that the general has taken prisoner?" Baylor asked after a few minutes of quiet.

"They will go to the capital, to Mexico City. I do not

know what will happen to them there," Carrasco said. "That is up to *las autoridades.*"

No one said anything else after this. The men began to drift away to their bedrolls by ones and twos. After a while, only Baylor was left, staring into the mottled coals of the dying campfire.

Two more days of easy riding brought the Rangers back to their station at Ysleta. As they rode through the villages of San Elizario, Socorro, and hamlets even smaller, a few of the local people stood at the side of the dusty trail, waving and smiling.

Hail, the conquering heros, Wiswall thought as he slumped in his saddle. When the Rangers had ridden out—was it three months ago, already?—these simple folks had acclaimed them as saviors: avenging angels who would sweep the demon Victorio from the earth. Now, through no direct action of the Rangers, Victorio lay dead on the plains of Chihuahua—thirsty, tired, sick of living—run to ground at last by the implacable forces of civilization. The good people of Socorro and San Elizario didn't have to worry about him any more. They and their alcaldes would have plenty of other worries soon enough, Wiswall guessed.

When they arrived back at Ysleta, Lieutenant Baylor found waiting for him a letter from the Adjutant General of Texas, informing him that he had received a promotion to captain. Coldwell's Company A of the Texas Rangers had been disbanded and its designation given to Baylor's command.

"Congratulations," Andrews told Baylor. "A well deserved promotion, in my mind."

"Thank you, James," Baylor said. He had an odd look on his face. "This means a rise in pay to the princely sum of one hundred dollars per month. Hardly a fortune. Still," he said, "it is honest work, and agreeable to me."

"When do you plan to head north?" Andrews asked Wiswall one evening in the bunkhouse, about a week after they had returned from Mexico.

Sitting on the edge of his bunk, Wiswall idly scratched Shep behind the ears as the dog sat on the floor in front of him. "I calculate the weather is getting cold up Leadville way," he said. "I expect the passes will be getting snowed in soon. I may wait until it starts warming up towards spring."

Andrews nodded. "Well. It may be pretty dull around here, now that we don't have Indians to chase."

Wiswall considered this. He looked at Shep. "What do you say, old boy? Are we going to get fat and lazy this winter, eating high off the hog, here in Ysleta?"

"Not like last winter, I hope," Andrews said. He dug in his pants pocket and pulled out a Barlow knife. He used it to scrape the dirt from beneath his fingernails. "Traipsing out into the middle of nowhere, getting our horses stolen, walking back here and freezing half to death along the way . . . Sitting in a warm bunkhouse sounds pretty good, all things considered."

Wiswall stared into the empty air above Andrews's head. "What do you make of those few Indians leaving Victorio's camp, the night we got there?"

Andrews finished the nails on his left hand, then shifted the Barlow to his other palm. "I don't know. I calculate they made it out, or Terrazas would've been sure to tell us."

"Yes, and that's another thing. According to Carrasco, another bunch left the next night, after

Terrazas had the place surrounded. So that's some more of them, unaccounted for."

Andrews paused his manicure and gave Wiswall a long, thoughtful look. "They liable to head back this direction, you reckon?"

Wiswall shrugged, still scratching the top of Shep's head. "Who knows? But I wouldn't start shopping for doilies to decorate your bunk. Not just yet."

Chapter 21

Toward the end of December, a rider dressed in the uniform of an officer in the *milicianos provinciales de Chihuahua* rode into the compound at Ysleta. After several inquiries for the whereabouts of "*Sargento* Gillett," the second-in-command of the station went to greet the messenger from the other side of the river; he waited on the front porch of Captain Baylor's house, the captain standing by his side.

As Gillett climbed the steps, the Mexican officer gave him a sharp salute and withdrew from the breast pocket of his uniform a parcel wrapped in oilcloth. He handed it to Gillett. "*Buenos dias, Sargento.* With the compliments of General Terrazas, I have brought back something I believe you were missing."

Gillett peeled back the layers of oilcloth to reveal the hunting knife, stolen from him months ago in the rough-country camp between Rebosadero and Borracho Pass. He cradled the blade in his palms; it had been carefully cleaned and sharpened; the metal held the smooth gleam of fresh oil.

"*Gracias, señor,*" Gillett said. "How did you find it?"

The militia officer gave a tiny smile. "It was found in the possession of the man who took it from you. He was seen using it to take scalps after our victory at Tres Castillos."

Gillett and Baylor greeted this detail with silence. "The thief has been punished," the Mexican said, after a while. "The General wishes me to tell you that he is sorry for this theft, and he personally asked me to restore the knife to you." He glanced down at the knife, still held in Gillett's open hands like a fragile relic. "It is a very good blade. I am sure that you missed having it." Gillett nodded. He looked down at the knife, then back at the officer. "Yes. Please thank the general for me." He gave a curt nod, then turned and walked away, down the steps and back across the dusty yard of the compound.

By the end of the year 1880, several reports of attacks in the open country around El Paso had made their way back to the Ranger station at Ysleta. An army patrol had been fired upon near Paso Viejo; an immigrant wagon train was attacked in Bass Canyon, with two passengers killed and another injured. And then, in a dawn attack at Ojo Caliente, south of the railroad camp at Sierra Blanca, a patrol of Buffalo Soldiers from Fort Quitman was wiped out except for a lone survivor. After two days in the mountains on foot and without food, the private staggered back into Fort Quitman and made a report to his captain. This ambush gained the Apaches all the patrol's equipment and baggage, and they apparently slaughtered and ate the soldiers' horses and pack mules.

Finally, just after Christmas Day in 1880, there was an attack on the stage in the notorious pass through Quitman Canyon, where Walde, the stage driver–turned Ranger, had barely escaped death the previous summer. The driver, a man named Morgan, and his passenger, a local gambler called Crenshaw, were presumably killed; no trace of their bodies was ever found. Suspicion began to circulate in El Paso that the two had somehow connived to rob the stage, then disappear and allow the blame to fall upon the renegade Apaches.

Inasmuch as such types of crimes fell squarely within the charter of the Rangers, Captain Baylor formed a patrol to investigate the stage robbery and determine, if possible, the true culprits.

Andrews, Wiswall, Baylor, Aniceto Duran, and ten other men left Ysleta on the cold morning of January 16, 1881, leading with them two mules loaded with ten days' provisions. Gillett stayed behind, in command of the Ysleta station while the captain was on patrol.

They picked up the trail of the attackers at Quitman Canyon and followed it southeast toward Ojo Caliente, where the Buffalo Soldiers had been massacred. After a hard day's ride, they came upon tracks of a number of unshod horses and mules and another mule with fresh shoes. Aniceto, scouring the ground around the trail, soon called out to Baylor. When the captain walked over to where the Tigua scout stood, he held a battered kid glove.

"I'd wager a week's pay that this glove belonged to Crenshaw, the gambler," Baylor said. "One way or another, we're on the right track here, boys."

After following the river bank for a time, the trail veered south into Mexico. With little hesitation, the Ranger party forded the river and continued tracking their quarry. Soon, they came upon signs of a camp that gave every evidence of having been made by

Indians. The next day's ride took them to the foothills of the Los Pinos mountains, the place where they had reluctantly separated from General Terrazas the previous October. Here they discovered another camp, along with the remains of a butchered horse and a pair of worn-out moccasins.

"Fellows, I harbor little remaining doubt that the stage was robbed by Apaches," Baylor said as they examined the scene. "Look how this camp is situated, with a wide view all around—just like their camp in the Candelarias."

As the captain and Aniceto continued to study the site, Andrews and Wiswall watched Shep going methodically back and forth across the place, his nose to the ground. He would walk a few paces and then dip his head down, taking several careful sniffs of a rock, a clump of muhly grass, the base of a creosote bush. Then, at a bed of brown and fallen leaves beneath a *frijolito* bush, he paused long: sniffing, then lifting his head to peer about before sniffing some more. With Andrews and Wiswall watching in curiosity, Shep stayed beneath the bush for perhaps three full minutes. When Captain Baylor called the remount, he took a final pull at the leaves, then came along with the party as it rode out—though not without a few backward glances toward the place he had just left.

More hard riding brought them to yet another place where their quarry had camped. Here they found a dead and partially butchered mule and also the top of a man's leather boot, which they surmised to have belonged to Morgan, the driver of the stage.

Aniceto soon pointed out to Baylor something even more worrisome: the sign of maybe as many as twenty mules and ponies that had recently come from the direction of the Candelaria range, to the northwest, and joined the trail of the riders they had been following from the site of the stagecoach attack.

"Well, it looks like General Terrazas may have left us more work than he anticipated," Baylor said.

Once again, Shep carried out his unusual canine reconnaissance of the campsite. He smelled his way back and forth across it before finding a particular spot—this time at the base of a limestone boulder—where he lingered, sniffing, looking around, and sniffing some more, until it was time to move on.

Riding near the end of the detail, Andrews and Wiswall discussed this latest observation in quiet voices. "I swear, it was like he was studying something," Wiswall said. "Like he was hunting for something specific, and when he found it, there he stayed."

Andrews frowned and shook his head slowly. "I've tried too many times to figure out what's going on between those two ears of his," he said. "I calculate he's got a burr under his saddle about something, though; that seems plain enough."

"Well, if the past is any indication, we'll learn what it is when he wants us to."

Andrews gave a sad little smile. "I do declare that I often wonder whether that dog belongs to us, or the other way around."

Wiswall chuckled softly. "You're still trying to work that out? I decided a good while back on that score."

After following the trail through some rugged canyon country, they camped that night on the Mexican side of the Rio Grande. Taking a cue from the Apaches, Baylor directed them to a place on a small, round bluff that overlooked the river. They would have a cold camp, he told them: no fires that might be seen by hostile eyes.

"Cold camp and no mistake, Cap'n," one of the men said. "In the morning, you might need to stretch me in the sun so I can thaw out enough to sit in my saddle."

Chewing on hardtack biscuits and jerky, the men huddled beneath their blankets as the quarter moon climbed into the eastern sky. In the steel-colored moonlight, Andrews and Wiswall watched as Shep made his way methodically around the camp, gleaning homage from each of the rough-and-ready men in the detail. Several of them tipped morsels of food onto the shepherd's tongue before giving him a fond pat. When he had received his due from everyone, he padded over and lay down between Andrews and Wiswall.

"What were you looking for today, old friend?" Wiswall said as he placed a strip of jerky in front of Shep. The dog snatched up the meat and made short work of it. "You're checking for something—or someone. Isn't that right?"

Shep licked his chops and turned to look at Wiswall for a few seconds before laying his head on his paws and closing his eyes.

"I guess that means he's not in the mood to discuss it tonight," Andrews said.

Wiswall smiled. He cradled his head in the seat of his saddle and stared up at the moon, climbing higher above the Rio Grande wilderness. *When he finds it, he'll let us know,* he thought.

Chapter 22

Liluye pulled the cowhide robe closer and leaned her head against Onawa's back. She wished the men would call a halt to this day's ride and let them gather wood for at least a small, hidden fire. It would feel very good to stretch her hands toward the blaze and feel the warmth licking along her arms and up to her face.

The horse struck a forefoot against a stone and stumbled. Liluye clutched at Onawa, and her robe fell down around her shoulders. The horse quickly recovered, but the cold air of winter had already slid against Liluye's skin. She gathered the robe again and closed her eyes, trying to imagine the warm earth during the time of the longest daylight. Liluye could not remember feeling warm a single time since they had left her grandfather in the camp at Tres Castillos.

She felt the sadness coming up in her throat again. She had known, when Onawa held out a hand to help her scramble onto the pony they would share, that she would not again see the face of Bidu-ya, whom the whites called Victorio. She could see the truth of it in his sad eyes, in the tired slope of his shoulders. For all of her young life she had followed him, had trusted him to decide what was best for the Chihenne, to find meat for them to eat and horses for them to ride. He had kept the women and children safe from the guns of the blue-coats and the brown-coated Mexicans. When her mother died on the reservation at San Carlos, her grandfather had kept her with him, had taken her along when at last they left that bad place behind. And now he was gone.

The men were angry. They wanted to fight the whites and Mexicans, to take revenge for the death of their chief. They had taken out their rage on the people traveling in the wagons through the canyon near the old fort, and again on the dark-skinned bluecoats at Ojo Caliente. She could still hear the screams of the stagecoach driver and the other prisoner they had taken in their latest attack. The men had peeled their bloody scalps from the tops of their heads while they were still alive.

But Liluye did not think the anger of the men would save them. She thought that they would only keep riding, riding, riding—cold and hungry and tired and always hiding from the whites and the Mexicans until, one day, they would all end in the same place as her grandfather. The anger of the men would not still the hunger. It would not turn away the cold wind.

The next morning the Rangers followed the trail of their quarry back across the Rio Grande into Texas. Just before exiting the riverside *bosque* of cottonwoods and hackberries, Aniceto darted aside to find a place where the Apaches had apparently cached some supplies in the loose soil near the river. They had left a tattered piece of white cloth tied to a pole that was wedged in some rocks on a nearby hillside.

"We can come back for this later, if need be," Baylor said after a few moments of study. "Let's press on after the Indians; dealing with them is more important than taking their stuff."

After following the Apaches' trail for a few miles along the north bank of the river, their track suddenly veered north. "I judge they're making for the Eagle Mountains," Baylor said, peering at the surrounding terrain and consulting his well-creased map.

"There's not much cover to the country up that direction once we get up out of the floodplain," one of the men said. "They'll see us coming from a long ways off, most likely."

Baylor nodded and frowned at the ground as he considered this information. "Aniceto," he said finally, "how long since they passed this way, do you think?"

The Tigua scout studied the tracks and thought for a while. "Two or three days. Maybe more."

Baylor stared toward the north, as if by great effort he might be able to discern the escaping raiders. "I think we'll risk it, boys," he said at last. "They're a couple of days ahead of us, and I wouldn't be surprised if they didn't have it in mind to get to the Guadalupes and then back into New Mexico. I think we can come behind them without too much worry about an ambush. But we'll keep a sharp lookout, no matter what. Let's ride on and do our best to close the distance."

It took them most of that day to cover the twenty or so miles of low but broken country between the river and the flanks of the Eagle Mountains. They came to the spring at the southern feet of the range when the sun was still two or three fingers' width above the horizon. Aniceto paced slowly around the spring and confirmed that the band had stopped here long enough to let their animals drink and to fill their water skins.

The Rangers made their camp around the spring

and set the watches for the night. Early the next morning, they took a trail that led them up toward the peaks of the range through a series of up-sloping canyons. On a shelf near the crest of one of the peaks, they suddenly rode up on a camp that gave every appearance of having been hastily deserted, and pretty recently so. Blankets, cowhide robes, and quilts were scattered about as if discarded in haste; two horses and a mule, partially butchered, lay off to one side, and the tongue of the mule was staked for cooking over a bed of coals that still retained heat.

"What do you make of this, Captain?" Andrews asked. He was standing beside a large pit lined with a horse hide. A dark green liquid filled the pit about halfway.

Baylor grinned. "Well, James, you have stumbled upon the source of the name for the Mescalero branch of the Apache nation. This pit is filled with cooked *mescal*, which they likely intended to cover with more hides, coals, and dirt and allow to bake until it was thoroughly fermented. Then they mix it with some water and boil it again. When it cools, they drink it like beer—but I'm told it packs a considerably bigger wallop than any beer you can buy in an El Paso saloon."

"I guess we must have interrupted a big party," Wiswall said, staring down at the murky concoction.

"Working themselves up into a war dance, most likely," one of the men said.

Aniceto was walking toward Baylor, holding out a boot top that matched the one they had found in Mexico, near the Sierra de los Pinos. "The mate to Morgan's other boot," Baylor said, taking the leather cylinder and turning it over in his hands.

"Here's a bag they made out of a man's britches

leg," one of the other Rangers said, holding up a piece of cloth sewn shut at one end with packing twine.

"I suppose this tells us pretty clearly about the fate of Morgan and his passenger," Baylor said. "I wonder if their bones will ever be found, so they can at least have a Christian burial."

"Looks like there's postal receipts and letters scattered around, too," Wiswall said, looking over the scene. "They finally got around to cutting open the mail pouches, I guess."

Aniceto cast about carefully, but he could not clearly determine which direction the band had gone as they left their camp. "Very cold last night," he said. "Colder up here. Hard ground. I cannot see the trail."

"What about going back down on the west side," Baylor said, "and starting back down by Eagle Spring, where we camped? We know they were there ahead of us; maybe we can pick up a line that way."

Aniceto nodded, and they remounted their horses and carefully descended the western face of the range. By midday they were back in the foothills, and the middle of the winter afternoon brought them back to the spring, where they were greeted by two men wearing the "cinco peso" star of the Texas Rangers, though they were not members of Company A.

"Lieutenant Nevill sends his greetings, Captain Baylor," one of the newcomers said. "We followed your trail here, and the lieutenant has ridden with the other six members of our detail to Fort Quitman to see if we could figure out which direction you had gone."

"Well, I am glad to have you and Lieutenant Nevill along to help us on this little excursion," Captain Baylor said. "We'll wait right here until he comes back, and then we can decide what to do next."

The next day, Nevill and his men rode into the camp, where Captain Baylor greeted them warmly. He introduced each of the men in the patrol, but when Nevill came to Andrews and Wiswall, he paused. Peering at them closely, he said, "I seem to recognize you two fellows. Haven't we met before?"

"Your memory serves you well, Lieutenant," Andrews said, shaking Nevill's hand. "You met my partner and me in San Antone, where you were kind enough to share with us your table at Link's chop house."

Nevill's eyes got wider, and a big grin crossed his face. "Why, that's exactly right! You're the two fellows who were trying to buy burros to sell back up in Colorado." He reached out to shake Wiswall's hand. "So, did you boys ever locate what you were looking for?"

"I'm afraid we only found two jackasses, Lieutenant," Wiswall said. "And they were us."

Nevill and the other men roared with laughter.

"If we had taken your advice more to heart, we'd have just headed back to Colorado without the burros and without making the acquaintance of Chief Victorio," Andrews said. "But on the other hand, we also would never have met Captain Baylor and these other friendly galoots. So, I guess in a way it all balanced out."

Nevill nodded, still chuckling. "Well, I'm glad you feel that way, boys. And I'm especially glad you're both still in one piece and able to tell the tale. I look forward to hearing it from you, while we're riding together."

Over a meal of beans and bacon, Nevill informed the group that he and his men had crossed the trail of the Apaches about six miles east of where they now sat. "From what we could tell, they were headed either for the Carrizos or the Sierra del Diablo," he said.

"That makes sense," Baylor said, nodding. "The last

time we had a clear trail from them, it was bearing up from the Rio Grande toward these mountains behind us. We found a camp up high here, but we couldn't pick up their trail from there. That's why we came back down here; to take another run at finding their tracks."

"Well, either the Carrizos or the Sierra del Diablo would be on their way to the Guadalupes," Nevill said. "I expect they're trying to make New Mexico and the Mescalero reservation."

"We had the same thought," Baylor said.

The two commanders compared their resources and soon realized that together, they had about enough rations for about five more days in the field.

"Why don't we press on with the pursuit?" Baylor said finally. "Either we'll catch up with them between here and the Guadalupes, or we'll get to one of the settlements up in the Pecos country and resupply from there."

Nevill nodded. "That sounds reasonable."

Baylor looked around. "All right, then, fellows. Let's take another couple of hours to rest and pack up, and then let's ride on. Maybe we can bring an end to this business in the next few days—once and for all."

Chapter 23

The trail of the Apaches led across the level country
north of Eagle Spring. Aniceto told Captain Baylor
and Lieutenant Nevill that the band looked to be traveling at a pretty good pace.

"I calculate they didn't realize we were as close on
their trail as we were," Baylor said. "Most likely, that's
why they broke camp back in the Eagle Mountains as
hastily as they did."

As the plain began to rise toward the foothills of
the Sierra del Diablo, they came to another place where
the Apaches had camped. Remains of a butchered
horse lay on the ground; while they were still a quarter
of a mile away, they saw coyotes slinking away from the
remains.

As they inspected the campsite, Baylor pointed and
said, "Now, that's the most ingenious thing I've seen in
a while."

The weather was holding bitterly cold, and the
snow that had fallen over the area over the past few
days still clung to the ground. In this place there was
no water, but the Indians had built a mud dam across
a narrow, shallow gulley. They had heated rocks in the
fire and rolled them into the gulley until they had a

natural trough full of sweet, cool snowmelt. They had then used this to water their animals and themselves.

"That's a trick I've never seen them use before," Lieutenant Nevill said. "You've got to hand it to them; nobody knows better how to make a living off the land than the Apaches."

"Not much of the horse left, and no traces of any meat lying around," Wiswall remarked. "I guess they butchered the animal, cooked as much of as they could, ate until they were full, and carried the rest along with them."

Led by Aniceto, with Shep trotting along beside him, the Rangers followed the trail that skirted along the western side of the mountains until it reached a point opposite the distinctive peak the Mexicans called *la Nariz*—the Nose. Here the trail led upward into the craggy folds and ravines of the Sierra del Diablo.

"They're making for Rattlesnake Spring, I'll wager," Captain Baylor said. "We'll have to go easy up these slopes, boys. Let your mounts pick their footing."

The patrol wound its way up through the craggy passes and came to the spring, where they found ample evidence of another camp.

"We are running out of daylight," Lieutenant Nevill said, squinting at the sky. "What about making camp here for the night and picking them up again at first light?"

Baylor nodded. "Men, divide up the sentry duty. I don't think our enemy is close at hand, but let's not get careless this late in the chase."

It was another cold camp. Wiswall had on every stitch of clothing he owned, and was swaddled in his blankets besides, and still he couldn't feel really warm. He wondered if there might be some way to induce Shep to sleep against his back, but he talked himself out of it.

Shep, meanwhile, as he had done at every occasion when the Rangers came upon a place where the Apaches had camped, carried out his olfactory inspection until he located one particular place that held whatever scent he was searching for. There he would stay for a long period of time, apparently until he had thoroughly satisfied himself that this was, indeed, the smell he sought.

Bright and early the next morning, the Rangers were back on the hunt. At midday, they struck yet another stopping place for their quarry, which told them that they were gaining ground on the Indian band. This camp seemed to indicate clearly, though, that the Apaches realized they were being tracked; it was located within a thicket at the head of a ravine, not out in the open on a height, as was their usual custom.

"If we had happened to stumble on them here, we certainly couldn't have got at them on horseback," Baylor commented. "And by the time we fought through the underbrush, I expect they'd have long taken to their heels."

At this camp, the Indians had slaughtered a deer; only the head and antlers remained.

"They hunt now," Aniceto said. "Must be careful; if they range far off the trail for game, maybe they see us."

By nightfall they had come upon another camping place. This one featured another pit dug for the roasting of mescal, and it was still warm.

"With any luck, we'll catch up to them before they eat all the mescal they've roasted up," Captain Baylor said.

"I thought you said they make it into firewater?" Andrews said.

"That's so," Baylor said, "but they also roast the heads of the plant, and when it is done up just right, roasted mescal tastes nearly as good as baked yams. Can't you smell that sweet aroma, coming from the pit?"

Andrews took a deep sniff and nodded. "Well, I guess you learn something new every day, if you're paying attention," he said.

"They left here this morning," Aniceto announced, after having a careful look around. "I think they don't know how close we are."

"Well, that's good news, if it proves correct," Nevill said.

The men had noticed more and more game sign the farther they rode, and they had seen several pronghorn, deer, and javelina skittering ahead of them, into the ravines. But they were under strict orders not to shoot at anything but an Apache; Captain Baylor wished for nothing to give away their location, now that they were getting closer to the object of the chase.

The energy and anticipation were palpable among the men that night. Many felt too keyed up to sleep, and sat on their blankets, carefully cleaning and oiling their weapons or inspecting their extra ammunition.

Once Shep had completed his peculiar examination of the site, he lay on the ground between Andrews and Wiswall.

"What do you figure? Tomorrow? The next day?" Andrews said.

Wiswall shook his head. "I don't know. I'm tired of trying to guess."

"Sometimes it seems like we've been worrying with Victorio and his people our whole lives, doesn't it?"

"Yes. Was it really just this time a year ago that we got mixed up with him in the first place?"

Andrews nodded. "Hard to believe." He gave Wiswall a wry grin. "What do you reckon we'll do with our spare time, once this is all over?"

"Figure out ways to spend more of our time in a warm place, for one thing," Wiswall said, tugging his blankets around his shoulders. "I don't know about you, but as far as I'm concerned, the virtues of the outdoor life are wearing damned thin."

Andrews gave a low chuckle. After a while, he said, "You still set on south California?"

Wiswall thought for a while. "I guess I am. But not before I see about Annie."

"I already knew that."

Wiswall stared at the ground between his boot heels for nearly a full minute. "What if I've set this all up in my mind, and there isn't anything else to it?"

"You really reckon that's likely?"

"Well, I sure as hell haven't gotten any replies to my letters, have I?"

"But the mail can be unreliable—especially out in these parts, with road agents and Indians and such."

"Maybe. I don't know."

"Well, I expect that here pretty soon, you'll have the leisure to set your mind at rest, one way or the other."

Wiswall nodded. "And I intend to. I just wish I felt more confident about the outcome."

"Well, there's one thing about it," Andrews said, leaning over to pat Shep. "No matter what, old Shep and I will always be here waiting for you, when you get back. Won't we, boy?"

"That's damned cold comfort."

Andrews laughed softly.

Chapter 24

"**L**ooks like they took another horse for the commissary department," Captain Baylor said, examining the carcass. "And look here, boys; the legs aren't yet stiff. Nor has the blood in the meat completely congealed."

They had been on the trail since first light, coming upon this latest Apache camp about midday.

"They eat snow for themselves, but their horses have no water here," Aniceto said, after a careful examination of the surroundings.

"How many horses does this make that they've killed and cooked?" Wiswall said. "At some point, if they keep on, won't they all be walking?"

"Remember that big track of stock we saw joining the trail way back south," one of the men said. "They're probably killing the ones that get too worn-out to ride and keeping the fresher mounts."

"That's how they have been able to stay ahead of us for so long," Baylor said, nodding. "When a horse can't be ridden, it gets eaten. And then they raid for replacements, as needed. They can move pretty fast that way, when conditions are favorable."

"They go northeast," Aniceto said, pointing.

"Trying to get to the Guadalupe Mountains, I'll warrant," Baylor said. "That's what I've thought all along."

"Do you reckon we could catch them out on the open plain, in between the two ranges?" Lieutenant Nevill said. "At the rate we're gaining on them, we're bound to come upon them pretty soon."

"We might," Baylor said. "Let's mount up again and follow this track out. Aniceto, lead the way."

By late afternoon, they were, by Captain Baylor's calculations, less than three miles from the northeast edge of the Sierra del Diablo. "This stretch of the range is fronted by cliffs and arroyos, all along the northeast edge," he said.

As they rode along near sunset, the trail of their quarry ran up the head of a brush-filled arroyo and over a high ridge on the other side. Reaching the top lip of the arroyo, Baylor called a halt. He stood in his stirrups, peering ahead and all around for several seconds. At that moment, a flock of doves veered overhead and vanished on the other side of the ridge.

"*Las palomas tienen sed*," Aniceto muttered. He looked at Baylor. "The doves go to water."

"Boys, I think our Apaches are on the other side of that ridge," Baylor said. "Wherever those doves are going to get a drink, that's where we'll find their camp. They'll want to be well-watered before crossing the plain between these hills and the Guadalupes."

"But if we cross that ridge now . . ." Nevill began.

Baylor nodded. "Exactly. We run a high risk of being seen. Let's camp here. And I hate to say it again, but no fires tonight. Let's not risk spoiling our surprise, either with firelight or the scent of smoke. Whoever stands the last watch before sunrise, make sure we are up and moving before the light comes up. I want to be on the other side of that ridge before sunrise."

True to the captain's order, the watch roused their companions in the pre-dawn dark. Before the eastern sky had turned from gray to pink, they were trailing down the eastern slope of the ridge, walking and leading their horses as Aniceto went in front, half stooped over, reading trail sign in the near-dark.

When they had gone along this way for about three-quarters of an hour, Aniceto suddenly held up a hand and squatted low to the ground. The patrol immediately froze. Looking around him, Wiswall saw the other Rangers' hands stealing toward their holstered sidearms.

Aniceto pointed. Ahead, perhaps half a mile away, a campfire flickered in the frigid dawn air.

Baylor signaled the men to back down below the crest of the small fold they had just climbed. Once they were hidden from possible sight of the Indian camp, he appointed five Rangers to hold everyone's horses. The rest would creep upon the Apache camp as quietly as possible.

Wiswall noted the disappointment on the faces of the five elected to stay with the mounts. *They'd better keep a sharp lookout, all the same,* he thought. *If some of the Indians escape our ambush, they're likely to run this way, and they'll not pause at killing anyone between them and some fresh horses.*

Led by Aniceto, Baylor, and Nevill, the attackers advanced in single file, staying low and moving carefully from one concealment to the next. Large outcroppings of needle-tipped yucca, called Spanish Dagger by the locals, grew pretty thick in the vicinity, and by staying behind these as much as possible, the Rangers were able to creep within about two hundred yards of the camp—still undetected, as far as they could tell.

Using hand signals, Baylor sent a detachment of ten men toward the left side of the encampment, with instructions to come as close as they dared, then wait for the sound of gunfire as their signal to engage. The other group would circle to the right and commence the attack on Captain Baylor's command.

Andrews and Wiswall followed Baylor and Nevill to the right; Shep padded silently between them. Remembering how Shep had barked at Rattlesnake Spring, just before Victorio's men had charged, Andrews kept looking at the dog, then at Wiswall. Wiswall discerned his partner's worry, but there was little to be done at this stage. He gave a little shrug as they crept along.

Shep, for his part, had his head up and was scanning the terrain with the keenest of interest. His nose wrinkled as he tested the air continually. Wiswall wondered if he was scenting whatever it was that he had been searching for at the abandoned Apache camps. Suddenly he had the thought: *not what, but who.*

When the first gunshot cracked, Liluye thought it was a green branch, bursting in the campfire. But then came a dozen or more loud bangs, and one of the men, squatting beside the fire, fell over with a bloody mass where the top of his head had been an instant before.

She sprang to her feet and ran, clutching the robe she had slept in. The world seemed to roar all around her and she saw only in blurs and snatches, like scenes lit by flashes of lightning during a storm on the prairie at night.

From somewhere behind her came yelling, but these were not the war cries of her people. She dashed headlong toward some rocks at the eastern edge of the camp, seeking a shield—any shield—from the death that spattered the ground on both sides of her feet.

When he had judged his men in the best possible position, Baylor had given a quick nod. The Rangers had poured a volley of rifle fire into the Indian camp. They reloaded and fired again, and then, at Baylor's order, they charged the camp, yelling at the top of their lungs.

Wiswall ran with the others. He saw one of the braves wheel around at the edge of the tree line on the east side of the camp and point a rifle in his direction. Wiswall fired his Winchester from the waist as he ran, and the brave disappeared. Wiswall didn't know if he had killed the man or if he had simply jumped into the trees. But he was still alive and uninjured, so he kept going.

Liluye cowered behind the rocks and looked back toward the camp. White men ran and shouted and fired their weapons. Her people lay dead on the ground.

Onawa ran toward the place where Liluye was hiding. Her eyes, wide with terror, locked with Liluye's. And then her chest burst open in a spray of crimson and she fell to the ground and rolled, as limp as an empty cowhide.

Liluye felt a scream starting in her throat, but her grandfather had always told her she must never allow a sound of fear to pass her lips. So she clamped her jaws shut against the scream, even as she stared in horror at what was left of the woman who had taken care of her when her grandfather sent her away.

Onawa was on her back, her arms flung wide. Her

cowhide robe was tangled around her legs. Her eyes stared sightless at the sky. One of the white men ran up to her and looked down at her before running on.

Liluye could not stay where she was; the whites would surely find her. They would kill her, as they had killed Onawa and the man by the fire.

Clutching her robe, she dashed out from behind the rocks, running for the tree line at the edge of the camp. If she could reach the trees, maybe she could hide from the whites until they were gone.

She had taken three strides when something struck her in the back, knocking her forward onto the ground. As she fell, she heard something buzz in the air where her head had just been; it sounded like an angry bee. She felt the wind from its passing blow hot against her cheek.

The air went out of her when she hit the ground. She realized that an animal had pounced on her as she ran; she felt its rough fur against her arm as she lay on the ground, dazed and struggling to draw air back into her chest. She tried to throw off the beast that held her down, but she could not; it crouched atop her and would not be moved.

Then, one of the white men was yelling. He was very close. Liluye swiveled her head enough to see him, running toward her with his gun in his hand. She closed her eyes. Now the bullet would come and she would be dead.

But the white man kneeled down beside her. He was still yelling, but it seemed as though he was yelling back at the other white men. He was waving his arm, as if trying to make something go away. He put his arms around the animal on her back. He was talking to it.

Liluye suddenly remembered the dog that had

come to her grandfather's camp beside the little lake at Tres Castillos. It was the night her grandfather had sent her away. He had talked to the dog, told it to watch over her. The dog had licked her hand.

And then she knew: the dog was on top of her. It had knocked her down to keep the white men's guns from killing her. It had kept its promise to her grandfather.

All of these thoughts crowded into Liluye's mind, even as the noise and shouting and gunfire kept on around her. The man kept talking. The dog continued to crouch on top of her. She closed her eyes again, not knowing what would happen now. She prayed silently to Usen and White-Painted Woman. She had tried to run away, but she had failed. She hoped that she was not about to die. She clamped her jaws tighter against the whimper of fear that was trying to burrow from inside her.

Chapter 25

Wiswall watched as the Rangers ran all around him, yelling and firing their Winchesters and Springfields at the fleeing Apaches. He kept a hand on Shep, who had the little girl pinned beneath him. Despite the noise and confusion, the dog never moved or even flinched.

Shep had made a beeline for the girl. Even before Wiswall realized what was happening, Shep had charged in from one side and knocked the child to the ground, likely saving her from the same violent death that had already taken most of her people. Now Shep kept his head down; his eyes roved ceaselessly over the field of battle. But he never budged from his protective position atop the Indian child.

"Is she what you were looking for?" Wiswall said, even as he realized the answer to his own question. Some bond, some understanding had driven Shep to seek out this little girl and then to interpose his own body between her and the hail of bullets coming from the Rangers' weapons.

Wiswall kept swiveling his head this way and that as he squatted beside Shep and the girl. Most of the other Rangers had passed his position by now; he could still hear intermittent rifle shots coming from the ravines below the campsite.

In a couple of minutes, Andrews came toward him, walking back from the north end of the scene with his Colt revolver in his hand. He stopped when he was about ten paces away, apparently registering for the first time what Shep guarded beneath his crouched body.

"Is . . . it's a child, isn't it?"

Wiswall nodded. "A girl."

"He's covering her. Protecting her."

Wiswall nodded again.

Andrews stared for perhaps ten full seconds. "Well, I'll be damned."

"He knocked her down and kept her still. Probably saved her from getting shot. Nearly got himself killed in the process."

Andrews shook his head. "I expect he's been following her scent since Tres Castillos."

"That's what I figure."

By now some of the men were returning from their pursuit of the Apaches. A few of them paused to look at Wiswall and Shep for a second or two, then went on with their inspection of the carnage. A couple of them began gathering up items that had clearly been plundered on the raids the Apache band had carried out since leaving Tres Castillos.

"Two good Winchesters, a Remington carbine, and a cavalry pistol," Andrews heard one of the men say, going through the captured goods. "And six US Army saddles. And that ain't near the end of it."

Three men straggled up out of a nearby ravine, and one of them was marching a woman ahead of him, the muzzle of his carbine in her back. She carried one hand in front of her, wrapped in a fold of her blanket that was soaked in blood.

Wiswall began trying to coax Shep off the little girl.

"Come on, boy, it's over now. You've saved her. Get up, now. That's right."

Slowly, Shep allowed himself to be eased to one side, and Wiswall put a hand gently on the child's back. "It's all right. No one is going to hurt you," he said. The girl looked at him, but if she understood anything he said, he could see no sign.

"I won't let them hurt you," he said. "But I need to see if you're hurt. It's all right."

He carefully lifted the robe she had bundled around her, scanning her clothing for any traces of blood. Her right moccasin was bloody on one side, and he feared the worst until he was able to gently peel it back; her foot was wounded, but it didn't look like a bullet hole. More like a rock, splintered by a rifle shot and propelled into her foot, he decided. It looked painful, but once cleaned and bandaged, it would heal.

"You can stay with me," Wiswall said to the child. "I'll take care of your foot."

The child's eyes, black as obsidian, never left his face. But her own face was as closed to him as if she were wearing a mask.

Poor child. You've seen more death this morning than many men see in a lifetime. It's a wonder you don't try to claw my eyes out with your bare hands.

"Is she all right?" Andrews asked, coming to stand beside Wiswall.

"She's got a wound on her right foot, but I think it will heal. Other than that, no marks on her that I can find."

"Looks like she made out better than that squaw over there," Andrews said. "That hand of hers is a mess."

"Can you stand up?" Wiswall said in the most gentle voice he could conjure. He put both hands on the girl's shoulders and tried to lift her. After an instant of hesitation, she pushed herself up from the ground. With Wiswall helping her, she got to her feet. She favored the wounded right foot. Her eyes roved around the scene, taking in the many bodies lying on the ground, along with the Rangers roaming to and fro, picking things up and putting them in various piles. Her face betrayed no expression whatever.

"She looks sound enough," Andrews said.

"I don't think she's suffered any physical wound, other than the foot," Wiswall said. "But merciful God above—what this child has just seen."

Andrews took a deep breath but said nothing.

The sounds of gunfire, which had gradually been diminishing in frequency and increasing in distance, stopped altogether. By ones and twos, the Rangers began returning to the campsite. One brought with him another child. Seeing the girl with Wiswall and Andrews, the Ranger brought the other young captive, a boy who looked to be about five, to where they stood.

"Reckon this 'un and yours know each other," he said. "Might as well let 'em wait together. Don't allow it'll hurt nothin'."

"You can leave him with us," Andrews said, putting a hand on the little boy's shoulder. "We'll keep track of him."

Shep reached his nose toward the Apache boy. As the child watched with the same expressionless, impassive eyes that Wiswall recognized from the girl, the dog gently sniffed his face. He licked the boy's hand once, then turned his attention back to the girl.

Just as Baylor and Nevill climbed the slope up from a bordering ravine, a young Ranger named Graham came storming toward Andrews and Wiswall. He aimed a rifle at the children and gestured angrily. "Get out of the way; I'm going to kill these damned Indian whelps."

Andrews held up his hand. "Now, settle down there, friend. These are just children; they can't—"

"By God, they'll grow up and turn into the same murdering savages that ambushed my brother and his wife in their wagon train in Bass Canyon. I aim to nip them in the bud."

Wiswall eased the girl and boy behind him and stood shoulder-to-shoulder with Andrews. "Well, now, I guess you're going to have to shoot my partner and me first."

Shep growled. Wiswall glanced down. The dog's hackles stood erect; his fangs were bared. It was the first time he had ever seen such behavior from Shep. He looked up at Graham. "And I reckon you'll have to kill the dog, too—if you can shoot quick enough to stop him before he rips out your throat."

Keeping his eyes on Graham, Andrews slowly reached down the collar of his shirt and tugged on the chain holding his locket. He pulled the bauble into view. "Do you know what this is?"

Graham still looked angry, but now he looked confused as well.

"This locket contains all that remains to me of my mother and father—killed by Kiowas seven years ago now. If anyone has a right to want to kill Indians, wouldn't you say I do?"

Wiswall remembered when Andrews had related this same story to Lieutenant Nevill the previous year on the occasion of their meeting at a chop house in San Antonio.

"But you can't think like that, Graham. You wear a badge. You represent a country with laws. Blood feuds aren't how the Rangers do things. Surely you can see that."

"Get out of the way, damn you!" Graham's eyes were wild again; the muzzle of his rifle trembled.

"Private Graham, calm down."

It was Baylor, stepping up to the young Ranger and putting a hand to his rifle. He pressed it away and down, then held it there in a grip of steel. "There will be no murder of innocent children, Graham. We've already killed two women and young ones, so bundled up in robes we thought they were braves. That's tragedy enough. No man in my command will shoot noncombatants—especially children—in cold blood."

The captain's eyes bored into Graham's until the younger man looked away.

"I'll take your rifle until you have a cooler head on your shoulders," Baylor said. "We'll deal with these children and the squaw according to the law, not according to revenge."

His jaw clamped and his eyes still averted, Graham released his grip on the rifle. As he walked away, Baylor shucked the cartridges from the Winchester onto the ground. He picked them up and put them in a pocket of his duster.

"Are we all accounted for?" Andrews asked.

Baylor glanced around the site. More men were returning from the surrounding trees and canyons. "Looks like everyone is back except two or three of Lieutenant Nevill's men," he said. "I think we'll finish loading up the army property and gather up the captured stock, then be on our way back to Ysleta." He studied the boy and girl for a moment. "It appears that Shep has taken charge of these two."

"For now, I guess," Wiswall said. "He knocked the girl down and crouched on top of her to keep her from being shot during the initial attack."

Baylor's eyes widened at this, and he took a longer, more careful look. "Well, that's . . . something." He looked again at Wiswall and Andrews. "We've got the ride back to the station to decide what's to be done with them, I guess. And the woman."

Chapter 26

A mong the stock captured from the Apaches were several army mules. These were soon loaded with captured saddles, along with bolts of calico and other goods taken from the raid on the stagecoach and other locations. The hide robes, pouches, and other goods of the Apaches were piled in the center of the campsite and put to the torch.

After making as much of a meal as possible with the meat they could find in the Apaches' stores, the Rangers saddled up and began picking their way down the southwest side of the Sierra del Diablo, aiming for the station at Eagle Spring. The recovered mules, now well laden with recaptured goods, strung along with the detail.

Wiswall had the little girl in the saddle in front of him, and Andrews shared his mount with the little boy. Neither of the children had uttered a sound since the raid on the camp, but neither did they offer resistance to anything that Andrews or Wiswall wanted them to do. Shep, instead of trotting ahead of the lead riders, as was his previous habit, stayed close to Andrews and Wiswall, with their young passengers.

The riders picked their way through the ravines and across the ridges of the mountain range, coming at last to the westernmost slopes that led down to the plain separating the Diablo range from the Carrizos Mountains, to the west. As the sun neared the horizon, they were well out into the flat country, but they managed to find a place that had decent grass and a few thickets of scrub—enough dead wood to make a good-sized fire. Captain Baylor called a halt, and the men began to make camp.

Wiswall set the girl down on the rock and signed to her that he wanted to look at her injured foot. She permitted him to remove her moccasin, and he did it as gently as he knew how.

The wound had just about stopped bleeding; it was crusted with dried blood but otherwise looked clean. Wiswall found the cleanest part of his bandanna and soaked it with water from his canteen. He gently daubed at the wound, trying to clean away the coagulated blood and grime before he bound her foot.

Watching her face, he said, pointing to himself, "Wiswall. William Wiswall." He tapped his chest as he said it.

She watched him, her eyes keen with understanding. But otherwise her face was as impassive as ever.

"William Wiswall," he said again. Then, he pointed at her and tilted his face with a questioning look. "Who are you? What do they call you?"

No response.

He started with himself again, repeating his name and tapping his chest, then pointed at her. Nothing.

"Well," he said, returning to nursing her foot, "I guess you don't want to talk. And I really can't say as I blame you, truth be told."

He cleaned off as much of the old blood as he could and then poured water from his canteen over the wound.

"I promise I won't let them hurt you," Wiswall said, carefully studying the foot. "You can stay with me, ride with me. And once we get back to Ysleta, I'll find somebody to take you in. A church, maybe."

He rummaged through his saddle bag until he found the spare shirt he had washed while they were camped at Eagle Spring, a few days earlier. He tore a strip from the shirttail and knelt down in front of the girl. He tore the ends of the material into strips and began winding it around the girl's foot, trying to make sure it was snug, without constricting circulation.

"Well, it's not exactly a surgical dressing, but maybe it will keep your hurt foot clean and let the healing start," Wiswall said. He tugged the ends of the strip toward each other and began tying them together with the strips.

"Liluye."

Wiswall quickly looked up at her. Those black eyes were fixed on him, though her face was still impassive. "Did you say something?" he said.

"Liluye." Slowly she raised a hand from her lap and tapped herself softly on the chest, twice. "Liluye."

Wiswall smiled. He nodded. "William," he said, tapping his own chest. Then, he pointed at her. "Liluye."

"Will . . . yum."

"That's right, that's my name. You can call me William. And I'll call you Liluye."

Shep padded up to them. He dipped his head and briefly touched the girl's hand with his nose. She looked at the dog a moment, then put her hand on his head. She looked at Wiswall. Slowly, she nodded.

Though the Apaches had been killed or scattered, Baylor still wanted sentries to take shifts throughout the night. Wiswall's lot fell during the last watch, from about four o'clock in the morning until sunrise. The man he was to relieve came and touched his arm at the appointed hour, and he shrugged out of his blankets and reached quickly for his duster; it was still very cold. He snugged his hat down on his head and buckled on his sidearm. Then, cradling his Springfield, he began making his slow rounds of the campsite.

The horses and mules were picketed to one side, near a thicket of catclaw. Just as the sky was turning gray in the east, Wiswall heard snorting and stamping. Instantly he hurried toward the mounts, and almost as quickly, he heard behind him the noise of the other men rousing and grabbing their hardware.

"One of them Apaches is trying to set us afoot!" said a voice in the darkness. "Mind the horses!" said another. There were sounds of thrashing, stomping feet, and the cocking of firearms.

Suddenly, from out of the darkness, a small shape flew at Wiswall and clamped itself around his right leg.

"What in the blazes— Liluye?"

It was the girl. Her face was buried in the side of his thigh, and her arms and legs were clasped around him as if he were the only thing afloat in a raging sea.

By now several of the Rangers were among the horses, reporting no signs of marauding Indians. "Likely a coyote sneaking through them bushes, yonder," one man said. "Spooked 'em a little, but they're all right."

Wiswall needed several minutes to pry Liluye loose from his leg. "What's wrong? Are you afraid they thought you were trying to steal a horse?"

Andrews came up to them. "Looks like you had an assistant for your rounds."

Wiswall shook his head. "She just came running up when the horses started to spook. Clamped onto me like white on cotton, and wouldn't let go. I think she was afraid someone would think she was messing with one of the horses."

Andrews pushed his hat toward the back of his head. "Well, I guess she thought if she was stuck tight enough to you, she wouldn't be likely to get shot."

Wiswall shrugged. "I guess."

After coffee and a few bites of dried beef, they rode on toward Eagle Spring, arriving there near sunset. Though the stage stand was by no means a grand lodging, it felt good to Andrews and Wiswall to sleep under some kind of roof, and in a room that could at least slightly contain the heat of a fire. The two partners kept Liluye and the little boy between them, and Shep placed himself on the floor at their feet. Wiswall enjoyed the soundest night's sleep he had found since leaving here for the Sierra del Diablo, almost a week ago.

The next morning, Lieutenant Nevill and his contingent said their goodbyes; they were bound east, back to their permanent posting at Fort Davis. Captain Baylor and his command aimed across the plain toward Fort Quitman, near the Rio Grande. They would then follow the river northwest until they came back to their quarters in Ysleta.

"I sent a note ahead with the stage driver who was leaving this morning," the captain remarked as they rode along. "Inevitably, when we're out on a patrol, someone in El Paso starts the rumor that we've all been massacred. I'm hoping that my note, which I've asked the driver to take straight to Major Magoffin, will save our families and friends some unnecessary heartache."

"I remember when we came back from Crow Flat, the vaquero we met on the way into town thought he was seeing ghosts," Andrews said.

Wiswall smiled at the memory. "I guess people will find something to talk about, even if they don't have anything to say."

"Yep. Bad news travels fast, and gossip travels even faster."

Wiswall studied the top of Liluye's head, bobbing as she rode along, seated in front of him. Who would get news of her? Was anyone still alive who cared if she lived or died?

Chapter 27

After another five days of easy riding along the river road, they were back in Ysleta. On the night after their arrival, the Rangers heard drums thumping and the sound of singing from the pueblo where the Tigua lived.

"I imagine that Aniceto has brought back news to the tribe's elders that those who killed his uncle Simon Olguin, along with the soldiers at Viejo Pass, are now dead," Sergeant Gillett said as he sat in a circle of other men in the bunkhouse. "They will be celebrating the avenging of the death of their kin."

"Victorio had a lot to answer for, that's sure," one of the other men said.

At this, Wiswall glanced over to the corner by his bunk, where Liluye sat. If the little girl noted the mention of her chief's name, she gave no sign.

She had uttered no sound since that day when he had bound her foot. Most of the time, her face was the same, void mask that she had worn since he had first laid eyes on her.

The only thing like feeling that she showed came when the nuns from Ysleta del Sur arrived to take charge of her and the little Apache boy. The kind-faced women smiled at the boy and he went with them willingly, as far as Wiswall and Andrews could tell. But as soon as Liluye saw them, she grabbed hold of Wiswall, as she had that dawn at the camp, and would not be pried loose.

"It's all right, Liluye," he said to her, trying to gently remove her grip. "They are here to help you." The nuns, too, spoke to her gently, trying to convince her. But Liluye would have none of it. She made no sound and her face stayed still, but her coal-dark eyes betrayed something like terror—or maybe rage. Finally, Wiswall shrugged and held out his hands to the sisters.

"I'm sorry. I guess she's just not ready yet. We'll keep talking to her; maybe we can bring her around."

The patient sisters smiled and nodded. They took the little boy away, their hands resting gently on his shoulders.

Andrews looked at Wiswall. "Well. Now, what?"

Wiswall studied Liluye for several seconds. "I can only think of one thing." He looked up at Andrews. "It might be the thing that saves us both."

Andrews tilted his head, a question on his face.

"Reckon you can look after Shep for a few days by yourself?" Wiswall said.

"I don't see why not. What makes you ask?"

"Someplace I've got to go. And now, I guess I'll have to take Liluye with me."

Wiswall held Liluye's hand as she stepped down from the train. He was dog-tired from the travel these last several days—first by stage to the Texas–Indian Territory line, and then by various railways—but it still did him good to see something on the girl's face other than the blank, emotionless mask she had worn at first.

She still would not speak, but she could not keep the curiosity about her unaccustomed surroundings entirely out of her expression. As he took his battered knapsack in one fist and Liluye's small hand in the other, he watched from the corner of his eye as she took in the sights and sounds of the Leadville passenger depot.

He had needed the patience of Job and the apparently inexhaustible persistence of one of the Tigua women to convince Liluye that a tub of hot, soapy water was not an instrument of torture. As he listened from behind the drape in the corner of the pueblo's central yard, the splashes and frequent exclamations of the Tigua woman told him, even without any words from Liluye, that the process was more difficult than it needed to be. And yet, in the end, Liluye came toward him with most of the campfire smoke, grease, and rawhide stink scrubbed off. She was dressed in a plain cotton pinafore, her hair was pulled back and braided. But she still wore her moccasins, and no amount of entreaty by either Wiswall or the Tigua woman could induce her to trade them for the second-hand lace-up boots that Gillett had borrowed for him from one of Captain Baylor's daughters.

Liluye had offered no resistance when they boarded the stagecoach or any of the trains; as long as Wiswall was next to her, she seemed content enough. She had stared out the windows as the country rolled by, and she had listened to and watched the other passengers, though she could not have understood any of their words.

A few people had given her a sour look, and when they boarded the train from Trinidad to Pueblo, Wiswall thought he was going to have to administer a thrashing to a red-faced man who made one too many remarks about "filthy savages" in a voice plainly intended to carry in Wiswall's direction. But the conductor arrived on the scene and asked Wiswall if he and his "young friend" wouldn't like to move to a nicer coach, and Wiswall allowed himself to be persuaded.

The Tabor Opera House was an easy walk from the depot down one of the main streets; it seemed the people in Leadville were as proud of the spanking new building as the mining magnate who had built it; everyone he asked seemed eager to point Wiswall in the right direction. He looked up at the handsome, three-story, brick façade and then turned his attention to the show bills plastered beside the ornate front doors.

Romeo and Juliet was the opera being touted, composed by some Frenchman with an unpronounceable name but apparently being performed in English, thank God. And then Wiswall read, in large, decorated letters: "Starring Miss Annie Milligan, 'The Songbird of the Rockies,' in the title role." Some tenor was listed next, but Wiswall's gaze was pinioned to the name of the singer playing Juliet and to the reproduced engraving that pictured Annie, costumed as Juliet, leaning against a vine-clad balcony as her Romeo mooned about below.

So she had come to Leadville, as she had said—and she was still here. Until the end of tonight's performance, at least, according to the notice on the sign.

Wiswall couldn't decide, in this moment, whether he was relieved or terrified. What if she was already married? But no. The name on the poster was still "Annie Milligan," as she had been known when he talked to her in Denver. *Maybe just a stage name and probably scant reason for hope,* he told himself. *But better than nothing,* he quickly thought in rebuttal.

Don't be such a fool, Wiswall. She probably threw all those letters in the trash—if she even got them. The notion made him want to take Liluye back to the station and buy a ticket on the next train headed back toward Texas.

He looked down at Liluye, and she was looking up at him. Her hand was in his, and her face, though still mostly impassive, held—what? The hint of a question? Confusion?

What in God's name is either one of us doing here, child?

"Are you hungry?" he said aloud. As if in answer, he felt his own stomach grind and growl. "Let's find a place to get something to eat. And then . . ."

And then I'm coming back over here to buy two tickets for tonight's performance.

Wiswall wasn't sure where that last voice had come from, but he decided to heed its advice. He looked around and saw a chop house across the street. Still holding Liluye's hand, he went toward it.

The seventy-two gaslights dimmed, and a hush fell over the audience. The conductor gave a downbeat with his baton, and the handful of musicians seated in the narrow passage between the front row of seats and the stage played the opening notes of the overture.

After a couple of minutes of violins sawing, a trumpet and trombone blaring, and the splash-boom of cymbals and a bass drum, the footlights blazed to life and the curtain rose to reveal a knot of costumed singers. From what Wiswall could catch, they were talking about the party that the Capulets were about to throw.

And then, to the accompaniment of the small

orchestra and the other singers, a man costumed as Capulet led his daughter, Juliet, onto the stage, whereupon she became the center of attention.

As soon as Wiswall saw Annie's entrance, he ceased to notice anything else. He even forgot that Liluye sat beside him in the dark. He forgot the other people, the orchestra, the cast onstage.

He watched her face and listened to the sounds coming from between her lips and he felt again, as he had that first night at the Denver Orpheum, that he had never in his life heard or seen anything as beautiful. As the high notes soared from her throat, he could almost imagine that his own spirit floated upward, carried by the beautiful resonance to hover in mid-air.

Time passed for Wiswall in an undifferentiated flow of color and sound. The only thing real and distinct in his consciousness was the figure and voice of Annie. And then, as the curtain rose on the second act, the lighting revealed her standing on a balcony at stage right, her eyes turned downward. To Wiswall, it seemed that she gazed directly into his eyes. He felt a shock run through his veins, from his scalp to the bottoms of his feet.

And then, with Liluye's hand in his, he was standing. He was walking down the sloped, carpeted aisle toward the stage. He was ascending the steps and walking onto the stage.

The conductor, staring wide-eyed, allowed his hands to drop. The musicians stopped playing. The audience watched in silence, and even Annie's expression had changed from the studied countenance of an actor playing a role to that of a woman facing a man who, from all evidence, was in some sort of a trance.

"Annie, it's me. William Wiswall. I talked to you

after your performance at the Orpheum in Denver. It was . . . I can't remember how long ago it was."

Her eyes widened. And still, no one else in the house made a movement.

"I wrote you, Annie. I wrote I don't know how many letters to you. I never heard back, so I didn't know if you got them, or . . . or if the letters made any difference to you.

"But I came to find you, Annie. I would have come sooner, but . . ." Wiswall glanced down at Liluye. The little girl stood beside him, looking up at him, and then looking at Annie, on the balcony, above them.

"I would have come sooner, but Andrews and I— he's my partner who went to Texas with me—we had to help the Rangers. And then we met Victorio. And there was trouble, and Victorio was killed, and then . . ." He looked down at Liluye again. "And now Liluye is with me. And Annie, Liluye needs you. I need you. And that's why I'm here."

The opera house was as silent as if no one had ever been there, as silent as if the place had never existed until this moment. Wiswall held Liluye's hand and looked at Annie. And she looked at him. And then she smiled.

"Of course I got your letters. I have every one of them, wrapped in a silk handkerchief in my room."

Wiswall's mouth dropped open.

"You said her name is Liluye?"

Wiswall nodded. "Her people were all killed, Annie. In front of her. And she's only said two words since. I—I don't know what to do for her."

Annie now looked at Liluye, and a tear trickled from her eye and made its shining way down her cheek. Wiswall wanted to touch that tear; he wanted to keep it forever, like a diamond in a velvet box.

"I think you are already doing for her everything there is to be done," Annie said. "I don't know how I could help."

Wiswall felt his shoulders sagging. For the first time, his eyes left Annie's, falling toward the floor.

"But I would give anything to try," she said. "William?"

"Yes?"

"Can we leave tomorrow?"

Somewhere in the back of the hall, in the upper reaches of the balcony, someone began to clap. The sound grew and spread until it enveloped the whole room. And then, people began to cheer and whistle. And then, they were on their feet.

Appendix

Shep In the Victorio War is based on true events. The documents and photographs that follow offer evidence to support the facts surrounding this important period in Texas history.

The Victorio War: A Brief Summary
by Thom Lemmons

Victorio (Bidu-Ya in his native tongue, "Holds His Horse") is believed to have been born in the Black Range of New Mexico in about 1825. He was a member of the Warm Springs Apaches, sometimes referred to as Mimbreños, though they called themselves the Chihenne. He became a trusted lieutenant of Nana, Mangas Coloradas, and Geronimo, and in time became known as a trusted leader.

Sometime around April 1877, the US government ordered Victorio and his people away from their ancestral territory to a reservation at San Carlos, in the Arizona Territory. Angered by being forced to live in an inhospitable and unfamiliar place, Victorio led a band of several hundred men, women, and children, along with horses and other livestock, off the reservation and back to their traditional homeland in southeastern New Mexico.

To maintain the band, Victorio and his men sometimes raided cattle and horses from outlying ranches and haciendas on both sides of the Rio Grande, and this soon brought them into conflict with both US and Mexican authorities. For the next three years, Victorio led the US Army, the Texas Rangers, and the

Mexican territorial militias on a wide-ranging chase as he continued his hit-and-run tactics. He raided mostly between Fort Davis and El Paso, and often crossed the Rio Grande to elude US pursuers. In the summer of 1880, Gen. Benjamin Grierson, commanding the 10th US Cavalry, made up of African American troopers the Indians referred to as "Buffalo Soldiers," decided on a strategy of denying Victorio and his people the use of watering places in the arid Trans-Pecos. Learning that Victorio had crossed the Rio Grande from Mexico and deducing that he was attempting to take his people to their strongholds in the Guadalupe Mountains, Grierson attempted to ambush Victorio at Rattlesnake Springs. After a battle lasting several hours, Victorio's forces withdrew, fleeing toward the Carrizo Mountains and back into Mexico.

In September, elements of the US Army and the Frontier Battalion of the Texas Rangers, stationed near El Paso, crossed the Rio Grande at the invitation of Mexican authorities in a coordinated effort to end the threat from Victorio, once and for all. To the reported consternation of the Rangers and others, the Mexican commander, Col. Joaquín Terrazas, ordered the US contingent back across the Rio Grande. Subsequently, on October 15, 1880, Terrazas and his forces fell upon Victorio and his people at a place called Tres Castillos, killing the majority of the fugitive Apaches with the exception of a number of women and children who were sent to Mexico City, essentially as slaves. Additionally, a few men, women, and children escaped into Texas, but they were later tracked and virtually eliminated by the Texas Rangers.

The article at right appeared in the Salt Lake Daily Herald on Thursday, October 21, 1880. It is interesting because of its sympathetic treatment of Victorio and his plight.

SALT LAKE DAILY HERALD, THURSDAY MORNING, OCTOBER 21, 1880.

VICTORIO, THE New Mexican Indian chief, has at last been killed, Victorio was a true hero, gazed at from the Indian standpoint, and from the white man's point of view was brave, daring and desperate, which also interpreted popularly means heroic. It wouldn't do to mourn over him, any more than it would do to regret that the British were killed or driven from the American colonies; but we can say that he was one of God's great creations, and the cause for which he fought was as dear to him as that which occasioned the American revolution—it was the cause of freedom. Victorio had been driven and crowded and cheated and lied to until he must have come to the conclusion that despite their professions to the contrary, the whites were a bad lot generally. Notwithstanding they claimed to love him and to desire his good, he naturally obtained different ideas from their conduct. Railroads were traversing his country and the civilization of the whites—his enemies—was steadily and rapidly hedging him in. Native instinct told him plainly that he must become a "good Indian"—that is to say, a dead one—or be no Indian at all. He chose to die an Indian, as the really superior Indian always does, and resolved upon selling his life for at least its full value, estimated according to the aboriginal rules governing transactions in human life. Over a year ago he and

his little band went upon the warpath, since which time they "murdered upwards of 400 persons," as the news telegram puts it. Whether or not it was "murder" depends altogether upon whether an Indian or a white man tells the story. Victorio, in the twelve months, has been in two territories, one state and two re publics, and has engaged in battle the armies of the two nations, as well as the militia and settlers. He fought against odds, and with all the advantages on the side of the enemy, until finally, reduced to the verge of starvation, his ammunition all gone, his little band decimated by hardship, exposure, incessant running and fighting, he has been captured and killed. Our neighbors across the border have the honor of striking the last blow and doing the final work of making of Victorio a "good Indian." Victorio was a genuine hero—one of nature's training. He fought foolishly, as many others have done, for a lost cause, but he fought bravely, first for what he understood to be his rights, and then revenge was the incentive that urged him on. Many a white general has won more glory and made more pages of laudatory history in a day, without getting within reach, if in sight of the battle ground, than Victorio could make and win if he were to fight as he has done for centuries; but no general was more heroic than he, and we question if any has been more conscientious. We don't mourn over him, but we rather like Victorio because he died an Indian for the reason that he could not live one.

The photo above has been widely circulated as Victorio (Bidu-ya, Beduiat; ca. 1825—October 14, 1880), but Apache scholar Robert N. Watt points out that Victorio was known to have a scar on his face that is not apparent in this photo. *Photo Courtesy of the Arizona Historical Society.*

There is no doubt, however that the photo above is Chief Nana, Kas-tziden or Haškɛnadiłtla (1800?—May 19, 1896). This is borne out by the stamp that appears on the photo. It reads: "Library of Congress copyright, May 17, 1884." *Photo courtesy of Laboratory of Anthropology, Sante Fe, NM.*

Above: Capt. George Wythe Baylor (1832—1916), Texas Rangers Company A, Sept. 1880—April 1885, and 1st Lt. of Company C, Aug. 1879—Dec. 1879; June 1880—Aug. 1880. *Photo courtesy of The Texas Collection, Baylor University, Waco, Texas.*
Below: James Buchanan Gillett (1856—1937), Baylor's Lieutenant at the time of the Victorio War. *Photo courtesy of the Texas Ranger Hall of Fame and Museum, Waco, TX.*

Above: Benjamin Henry Grierson (1826—1911) organized and led the Buffalo Soldiers of the 10th Cavalry Regiment from 1866 to 1890. *Photo courtesy of the National Park Service, Fort Davis National Historic Site.* **Below:** Coronel Joaquin Terrazas y Quezada (1829—1901) is best remembered in Mexico for defeating of Victorio. *Photo courtesy of the Benson Latin American Collection at the University of Texas, Austin, TX.*

Above: First clear sight of Tres Castillos.
Below: The south end of the north hill at Tres Castillos looking over a full laguna.
Both photos are used courtesy of Robert N. Watt

Acknowledgments

Almost 140 years have lapsed since nine Texas Rangers rescued a stranded, starving dog from an abandoned stage coach station at Crow Flat Spring, 100 miles east of El Paso in the rugged heart of Mescalero Apache country. That story appears in *Faithful Shep: The Story of a Hero Dog and the Nine Texas Rangers Who Saved Him.*

Shep, in the anomalous position of having participated in a hard reality on the Western Frontier during the early 1880's, was allowed animation as a hero dog of historical fiction by three people who believed in him. They are:

- Paul Ruffin (1941-2016), founder and Director of Texas Review Press, who agreed to publish the book because he loved "dawgs" as much as Rangers. (Best of all, Ruffin recommended Thom Lemmons as copy editor.);
- Thom Lemmons, the unrivaled, nonpareil editor who so spiritedly responded to my call for help with writing of such poignancy and simple beauty that only the hardest of hearts would not melt for the dog; and
- Kim Davis, editor and interim Director of Texas Review Press, who has mantled TRP with the same leadership perseverance and homing instinct Paul envisioned for tomorrow's successful publications.

Don DeNevi
Spring, 2018